IRISH
LEGENDS

Irish Legends

Iain Zaczek

Gill & Macmillan

Published in Ireland by
Gill & Macmillan Ltd
Goldenbridge
Dublin 8
with associated companies throughout the world

First published in Great Britain in 1998 by Collins & Brown Limited

ISBN 0 7171 2751 6

Conceived, designed and edited by Collins & Brown Limited

Editorial Director: Sarah Hoggett
Editors: Katie Bent and Kate Yeates
Picture Research: Katie Bent
Art Director: Roger Bristow
Designer: Alison Verity
Cover Design: Julia Ward-Hastelow

Reproduction by HBM Print, Singapore
Printed and bound by De Agostini, Italy

Contents

Introduction

Ireland's legends provide us with a truly unique and captivating insight into the fantasies, hopes and dreams of an ancient race. This vision is all the more refreshing, because it is comparatively unaffected by the two dominant influences on early European thought – classicism and Christianity. Ireland never became a province of the Roman Empire and, as a result, the folk memory of its earliest peoples was allowed to survive in a remarkably pure form. The Church, of course, played a much greater role in Ireland's early history, and Christian scribes were ultimately responsible for transcribing many of the ancient myths. Even so, this process occurred at a time when the battle against paganism was a distant memory, thereby removing the chief incentive for tampering with the original content of the legends.

Before the spread of Christianity, the ancient tales were passed down by oral means. There was a rather basic form of writing in Ireland, known as ogham, but this seems to have been used mainly for ritual purposes. A few inscriptions on stone have survived, but there is nothing to suggest that attempts were ever made to copy down the stories in ogham. In the light of this, the survival of the Irish legends is truly remarkable, testifying to the efficiency of the system which the Celts employed.

All branches of learning were transmitted orally from generation to generation. The officials entrusted with this crucial role were the filidh, a semi-mystical class of poets. At first, they were seen as something akin to magicians, possessing the gift of foresight and the ability to raise great storms and mists. In time, some of the duties of the filidh passed to the druids and the brehons (lawgivers), leaving them to concentrate on poetry and philosophy. Even so, they retained a privileged position within the community, often acting as royal advisors. The details of their training are far from clear, though there are indications that it might have lasted for as long as twelve years.

Certainly, the amount of material which the filidh were expected to commit to memory was impressive. One early manuscript, the Book of Leinster, recorded that each fili ought to be able to recite three hundred and fifty tales; that is, two hundred and fifty *príomscéalta* (main stories) and one hundred *foscéalta* (secondary tales). These stories covered a wide range of subjects, including *Catha* (battles), *Eachtraí* (adventure-journeys), *Tána* (cattle raids), *Físi* (visions), *Tochmarca* (wooings) and many others. Over the course of time these different strands became woven together, so that the original theme is not always clear.

It seems probable that the filidh achieved their herculean feat by learning the bare bones of each narrative and then extemporizing the rest. This would explain why the surviving versions are so consistent in their general outline, but vary so much in their details. It would also account for the ramshackle structure of many of the tales. All too often, a compelling storyline is interrupted by a digression into a related myth or a complex genealogy. Sometimes, this may simply reflect the stamina of the speaker. On occasions, there are lengthy lists and descriptive passages, where the poet warms to his task of evoking fine armour and jewellery, or

the wonders of a magical land. These, in turn, may be followed by a disappointing anticlimax, when the storyteller begins to grow tired.

By the same token, it is not uncommon to find inconsistencies within groups of tales. The various cycles are made up of disparate collections of stories and do not form a unified whole. Consequently, it was possible for Cú Chulainn to swear undying love for Emer in one story, carrying out a daunting series of labours in order to win her hand, and then treat her with complete disdain in a separate tale. The same is true of the overall structure of the sagas. By rights, the narrative should reach a crescendo with the decisive battle at the end of the Ulster cycle. Instead, this episode pales into insignificance beside an earlier encounter between Cú Chulainn and Ferdia.

Equally, it is important to stress that the principal legends were not the relic of a single age or culture. It is possible to deduce the approximate period when many of the stories are set – the first century BC in the case of the Ulster cycle and the third century AD in the Fionn cycle – but this should not imply that they were composed during the same era. Rather, the cycles were built up over the course of many centuries, with each generation adding to or modifying the tales.

Several authorities, for example, believe that the enchanted palace in *The Curse of the Quicken Trees* was originally part of an adventure in the Otherworld and was only relocated to Ireland at a relatively late stage. Similarly, there are two distinct traditions which account for Finn's powers of divination. In one version, he gains this ability after eating a magical salmon, while, in a different tale, he acquires the same gift after catching his thumb in the door of a Sidh. According to this second version, Finn induces his prophetic visions by sucking his thumb.

The accumulation of new stories continued long after the spread of Christianity, as did the influence of the filidh. Indeed, they acquired new responsibilities after the decline of the druids, and are thought to have remained active in Ireland until as late as the seventeenth century. Even so, the practice of transcribing the stories was well advanced by the Middle Ages. No one is sure exactly when the process was introduced, though some experts believe it may have begun as early as the seventh century, citing linguistic evidence to support their claims. Despite this, none of the surviving manuscripts dates back further than the eleventh century.

The most important collections of mythological material are preserved within three priceless volumes: the Book of the Dun Cow (Leabhar na h-Uidhre), the Book of Leinster (Leabhar Laighneach), and the Yellow Book of Lecan. Each of these books is like a miniature library in its own right, containing a rich miscellany of legal, religious and literary texts.

The Book of the Dun Cow is the oldest of the three volumes. It was compiled at the monastery of Clonmacnois in around 1100, largely through the efforts of a monk named Maelmuire. The book features a version of *The Cattle Raid of Cooley*, along with several other stories from the Ulster cycle. In addition, there are brief extracts from both the mythological and Fionn cycles, as well as the entire retelling of the Voyages of Maeldun and Bran. These legends are interspersed with sections of

Nennius's 'History' and a number of poems attributed to St Columba.

The Book of Leinster contains an even more diverse selection of material. The manuscript was transcribed by Finn Mac Gorman, a bishop of Kildare, and completed before his death in 1160. It provides a different, Middle Irish reading of *The Cattle Raid of Cooley*, which is more extensive but less powerful than the Dun Cow version.

The Leinster volume also has a few extra stories, among them *The Exile of the Sons of Usnach*. Alongside these, there are lengthy catalogues of kings, saints and genealogies, together with poems and documents that relate specifically to Leinster. The volume also features versions of the Book of Invasions and the *Dinnsenchas* (the Lore of Prominent Places), both of which have strong links with the legends.

The Yellow Book of Lecan is much later, dating from the late fourteenth century. Unlike the other volumes, this manuscript was produced for a private family, the O'Dowds, the chieftains of the Hy-Fiachrach clan, and was compiled by their hereditary scribes. Despite its comparatively late date, this contains the earliest-known version of *The Cattle Raid of Cooley*, together with a number of other tales.

The very fact that the legends were transcribed at all is evidence of the importance that was attached to them, both by the lay and Christian communities. Producing manuscripts was a costly and time-consuming business, reserved exclusively for the most precious of documents. If further proof were needed, this is confirmed by the reputations of the manuscripts themselves. The Book of the Dun Cow, for example, was virtually a holy relic. Legend had it that the young St Ciaran (c. 512–c. 545) had travelled with a favourite cow, both when he was a student and when he came to found the monastery of Clonmacnois. According to tradition, the skin of this same beast was then preserved for more than five centuries, before being used as parchment in the Book of the Dun Cow. At a later date, the manuscript was stolen from the monastery and had to be 'forcibly recovered from the men of Connacht' by a son of Niall the Rough. Clearly, a book that had such saintly connections, and which could become the pretext for a war, would never have been used to record information that was either trivial or routine.

TALES OF THE GODS

The earliest Irish legends deal with the country's ancient gods: the Tuatha Dé Danaan (the People of the Goddess Danu), a race of divine beings who arrived in Ireland during the prehistoric period. In the myths, these primordial times were described in terms of a series of conquests. Annalists later compiled the disparate accounts into a so-called Book of Invasions, which was traditionally placed at the start of the manuscript anthologies. Both the Dun Cow and Leinster manuscripts open with their version of these conquests.

The Book of Invasions normally listed five specific groups of invaders: the Partholónians, the Nemedians, the Firbolg, the Tuatha Dé Danaan and the Milesians. The first four of these were described as gods, although the powers of the Danaans were evidently much weakened. This eventually led to their defeat by a race of mortals, the Milesians. The latter may have had some historical basis, since they were hailed as the ancestors of the Gaels, a genuine Celtic people.

The earliest invaders played no significant role in the legends, leaving the limelight to the Tuatha Dé Danaan. Storytellers related how they came to Ireland from their four magical cities: Falias, Murias, Finias and Gorias, bringing their greatest treasures with them. From Falias came the Lia Fáil, the coronation stone of the high kings at Tara; from

Murias, they brought the Dagda's cauldron, the feasting-vessel which never ran short of food; and, from the remaining cities, they transported Lugh's invincible sword and a magical spear.

The Danaans won two formidable victories at Mag Tuireadh (the Plain of Pillars). In the first of these, they vanquished their predecessors, the Firbolg, although their leader, Nuada, lost his hand in the process (see feature on page 107). At the second, they overcame a tyrannical race of sea pirates, called the Fomorians. This is the battle won by Lugh, at the start of *The Punishment of the Children of Tuireann*.

Their next source of conflict came from the Milesians. At first, this appeared to be an uneven contest. When the newcomers mounted their initial challenge, for example, the Tuatha Dé Danaan simply agreed to surrender, provided that their foes made no attempt to take them by surprise. Delighted at the prospect of such an easy victory, the Milesians accepted these terms and withdrew to an agreed point – the length of nine waves from the Irish shore. When they turned their ships around, however, they discovered that the Danaans had used their mystical powers to draw down thick mists and terrible storms. Soon, Ireland was lost from view and their fleet was scattered to the farthest corners of the Western Sea.

Despite setbacks of this kind, the Milesians eventually overcame the magical wiles of their opponents, defeating them at the crucial Battle of Tailltin. After this humiliation, the gods retreated to their Sidhe, leaving Ireland to be ruled by the world of men. They retained an interest in their old haunts, however, frequently returning to meddle in the affairs of their former subjects.

Most of the mythological tales are set against the backdrop of this dual landscape, alternating between the land of mortals and the domain of the gods. Often, it can be hard to distinguish between the two. In *The Wooing of Etain*, for example, the status of the rival suitors may not be immediately apparent. Eochaid Airem is a mortal king, while Midir is a member of the Danaans, and his home at Brí Leith (the Mound of the Grey Man) is actually

one of the Sidhe. Similarly, in the story of the children of Lir, the essence of the tragedy lies in the fact that they are banished from their fairy homeland and trapped in the world of humans.

Although they are set in prehistoric times, the mythological tales reflect many aspects of later Irish society. There are frequent hints, for example, of the Celtic belief in the power of the triad. Some deities – most notably the craft-gods and the war goddesses – were conceived as trinities and might even be depicted with three faces. On a more mundane level, this is also why numbers are often expressed in batches of three (thrice twenty, thrice fifty, and so forth) and why the stories about the various offspring of Lir, Tuireann and Usnach all feature three children. Significantly, in each of these tales, only one of the characters emerges with any real identity, while the remainder are – quite literally – just making up the numbers.

Another facet of early Irish society is revealed in the curious role of poets and satirists. It is clear from all branches of the legends that these figures were accorded special privileges. As a young man,

Finn was eager to learn the art of poetry from Finnegas, knowing that it would help him to be reconciled with both the king and his father's enemies. Similarly, the sons of Tuireann managed to gain access to a number of royal courts by posing as poets. In other cases, there are subtle hints that fear, rather than respect, lay behind this favour. This would explain why, in the story about the sons of Usnach, Conchobar seems unable to prevent a female satirist from visiting Deirdre.

This fear was genuine enough. Celtic princes placed a high value on their reputation for generosity and hospitality. Anyone who fell short lay himself open to the threat of being satirized. This was more than just a matter of shame and public disgrace. The consequences could be dire, for no king could rule in Ireland if his reputation was less than perfect. By tradition, the very first Irish satire was directed against Bres, one of the leaders of the Tuatha Dé Danaan. A poet called Corpry lampooned him for his lack of hospitality and this, it is said, lost him his throne. In some cases, the satire worked like an enchantment. One legend tells how Caiér, a king of Connacht, was satirized unjustly by his nephew. Even though the accusations were false, the poisonous verses still produced three blisters on Caiér's face, forcing him to resign, since no king with a physical blemish could hold office. In the light of such poetic sanctions, it is hardly surprising that Irish kings were wary of offending any man of letters.

THE ULSTER CYCLE

In the tales of the Ulster cycle, we enter a different world. The gods have receded into the background and, in their place, an aristocratic warrior caste has taken centre stage. These heroes revel in fighting and are driven by a need for personal glory. They may sometimes perform superhuman feats, but these are attributed to magnificent weapons or to a battle-frenzy, rather than to divine powers. Even so, the dividing line is often a thin one. Cú Chulainn, although mortal, is still the son of a god and could easily be defined as the human equivalent of Lugh.

Conversely, Medb is a former goddess, reduced to the rank of a queen. In her divine role, she symbolized sovereignty and fertility, and had participated in ritual matings with the high kings at Tara. None of these roles is apparent in the *Táin*, however, although the squirrel and bird, which perch on her shoulder, may hint at her earlier shape-shifting powers.

It is doubtful whether the characters or events portrayed in the cycle were based on reality, but the setting has a definite ring of authenticity. The Ulstermen did indeed have their capital at Emain Macha, now identified with the archaeological site of Navan Fort, not far from Armagh. More than this, the military and social details in the *Táin* accord very closely with some of the accounts set down by classical authors. They noted how the Celtic princes used to fight in chariots, charging round the battlefield in an apparent frenzy; they commented on the bravery of their warriors, who seemed to lack all fear of death and who delighted in challenging their foes to single combat; above all, they lingered over the gory details of their head-hunting practices.

The Ulster cycle also reflected certain aspects of social organization. The Celts were a group of tribes, rather than a single, united people. These divisions often proved a weakness, particularly in times of warfare, but the system was strengthened by a complex system of fostering. Children would often be reared in the household of a neighbouring druid or chieftain, even if their blood-parents were still alive. In theory, these broader ties helped to bind the community together. In the *Táin*, there is also an implication that a foster-son will absorb the skills of his foster-father, whether in fighting, divination or the art of kingship.

On a rather more enigmatic level, the tales of the Ulster cycle offer some insights into the *geis*, an unusual form of taboo. This curious institution, which was part-curse and part-social obligation, placed heavy restrictions on the actions of the individual. For to ignore a *geis*, was to risk bad luck, ostracism from the tribe, or even death. Accordingly, in many episodes of the *Táin*, Cú Chulainn delayed the Connacht army by inscribing a *geis* in ogham letters on a stone or tree. In most cases, this prohibited his opponents from proceeding any further, until they had carried out some specified feat. A *geis* could also be used as a form of enchantment. In the story of the sons of Usnach, for instance, Deirdre employed one to compel the reluctant Naoise to elope with her, much against his better judgement.

THE FIONN CYCLE

Until the Celtic Revival, which was spearheaded by W B Yeats and Lady Gregory at the start of the twentieth century, the stories of Cú Chulainn and the cattle raid of Cooley were only familiar to a fairly limited audience. The tales of Finn and his companions, on the other hand, were known throughout Europe, having earned a prominent place in the Romantic movement.

This pre-eminence did not occur until a comparatively late stage. Initially the character of Finn, like that of Cú Chulainn, probably developed out of the solar cult of Lugh. This is underlined by the meaning of his name, 'the Fair One'; by his battle with the fire demon, Aillen; and by the importance of the episode where he burns his thumb. Legend soon placed him at the court of Cormac Mac Art, a genuine, third-century king of Tara, but very few stories were associated with him. Out of the three hundred and fifty filidh stories listed in the Book of Leinster, Finn figured in just five.

The shift in emphasis appears to have begun at the end of the twelfth century, partly perhaps because of a change in taste, following the Anglo-Norman invasion of Ireland in 1175, and partly because of the growing vogue for Arthurian romances. In the minds of contemporaries, the warriors of the Fianna evoked obvious comparisons with the knights of the Round Table. Some looked for even closer links. There was a tradition, for example, that Camelot was derived from the name of Finn's father, Cumhal. Soon, the legends in the Fionn cycle were expanding rapidly, eclipsing the other, more ancient strands of Irish mythology.

Because the stories of Finn and the Fianna were composed over a lengthy period of time, there are striking disparities within the cycle. It is difficult, for instance, to reconcile the fresh-faced heroism of the young Finn with the older, jealous husband, who harries Diarmaid and brings about his death. More glaring still are the later legends, which portrayed the Fianna as giants. Evidence of this can be found in the story of *Oisin in Tir na nÓg*, where the Irish seem like pygmies to the returning warrior, and also in the legend of the Giant's Causeway. Here, by tradition, the giant in question was Finn, who built a fairy bridge joining the Irish coast with Fingal's cave, on the island of Staffa.

Finally, there is a marked change of tone in some of the tales. Where Cú Chulainn and the Ulstermen had been whole-heartedly involved in their adventures, the deeds of the Fianna were often viewed from a Christian perspective. Consequently, several tales have an elegiac flavour, as the aged warriors look back with a certain nostalgia to the wild hunts of their youth and the joys of vanished paganism.

IN PRIN
CIPIO
ERAT VERBUM
ET VERBUM ERAT
APUD DM ET

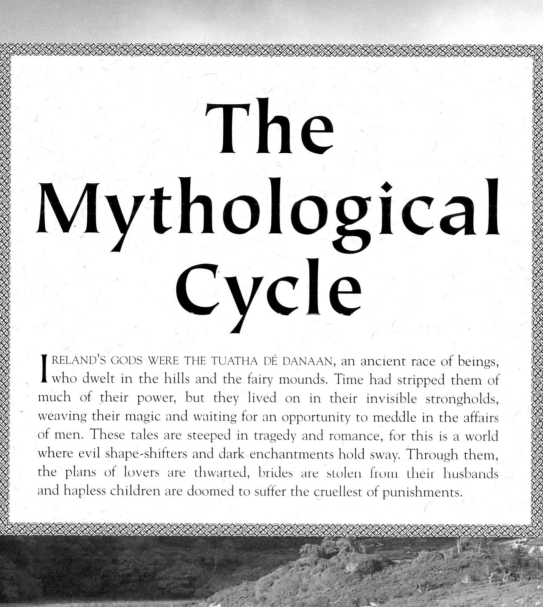

The Mythological Cycle

IRELAND'S GODS WERE THE TUATHA DÉ DANAAN, an ancient race of beings, who dwelt in the hills and the fairy mounds. Time had stripped them of much of their power, but they lived on in their invisible strongholds, weaving their magic and waiting for an opportunity to meddle in the affairs of men. These tales are steeped in tragedy and romance, for this is a world where evil shape-shifters and dark enchantments hold sway. Through them, the plans of lovers are thwarted, brides are stolen from their husbands and hapless children are doomed to suffer the cruellest of punishments.

The Taking of the Fairy Mound

Now the chief of Ireland's gods was the Dagda, the giver of life and the bestower of all bounties. With his mighty right arm, he wielded the club of creation, one end of which brought death and perdition to the living while, with the other, he could restore dry bones to life and put new light into the eyes of a corpse. The Dagda took as his palace the Sidh of Brug na Bóinne, the finest of all the fairy mounds in Ireland. Here, he kept his magic harp, which flew into his arms upon command. Here, too, was his fabled cauldron, with its inexhaustible supply of roast boar's meat, and his stock of Goibhniu's ale, which rendered the drinker immune from all sickness and death. Lucky the feaster who came to such a table.

While residing in this pleasant spot, the Dagda's gaze fell upon a beautiful water spirit named Boann, the protectress of the River Boyne, and he desired to possess her. Boann returned his favour and would have lain with him, but she feared the wrath of her husband, the powerful Lord Elcmar. So, sensitive to her wishes, the Dagda sent his rival away on a mission, bidding him take a message to Bress, son of Elatha. Then he wove a spell upon the hapless husband, causing time to stand still for him. For the space of nine months, Elcmar felt no thirst or hunger, and perceived neither the brightness of the day nor the blackness of the night. During his absence, Boann conceived and bore a child, a son named Oenghus, and the Dagda carried him off and fostered him in the household of Midir the Proud. And when Elcmar returned home, he suspected nothing of this. For, it seemed to him that he had only been parted from his wife for a single day.

Oenghus was reared at the house of Midir and, such was the favour shown to him, he believed that he was the son of this great lord. This conviction remained with him until his ninth year, when the truth was revealed. He was out on the playing fields, sporting with the youths of the neighbourhood, when he fell into an argument with Tríath, son of Febal, a member of the defeated Firbolg people. Tríath spoke to Oenghus, addressing him as an equal, and the youngster took offence at this.

'Hold your tongue,' said Oenghus angrily. 'It is not fitting that the son of a slave should treat me with such familiarity.'

But Tríath was unabashed. 'It is no less fitting,' he replied, 'that such words should be spoken by a mere foundling, who is ignorant of his own father and mother.'

Shocked by this news, Oenghus hastened to Midir and demanded to know the facts. 'It is true that you are no son of mine,' the latter admitted, 'but your father is the mighty Dagda, one who is even more worthy of your respect.'

Oenghus was appeased by this, though he was determined to suffer no further mockery from a child of the Firbolg. His father must be made to acknowledge him and grant him his birthright. With this in mind, he travelled to see Manannán Mac Lir, a potent sea god and a master of trickery. Manannán advised him to go to his father at the festival of Samhain, for this was the magical season, when great changes could be wrought in the fortunes of both gods and men. At this auspicious moment, he was to beg the Dagda to grant him the tenancy of Brug na Bóinne for the space of a night and a day. For his part, Manannán pledged to use his wily arts so that the Dagda could not refuse.

As it was commanded, so was it done. Oenghus journeyed to Brug na Bóinne and asked his father to give him possession of the fairy mound for a night and a day. The Dagda gazed fondly on his son and, swayed by the enchantments of Manannán, he readily agreed to yield up his palace on those terms.

He departed immediately and, for the space of a night and a day, Oenghus held the kingship of the fairy mound.

At the end of the allotted time, the Dagda came again to Brug na Bóinne and requested the return of his palace. But Oenghus refused his father, explaining that he was now the rightful owner of the mound. He had been granted lordship over it for a night and a day and, since the passage of time consists of nothing more than night and day, following each other in endless succession, he was now master of the palace for all eternity. Then the Dagda realized that he had been tricked. He went away, taking his household and his people with him, leaving Oenghus to enjoy Goibhniu's ale and the feast that never failed.

Oenghus in Love

Oenghus was asleep in his bed one night, when a beautiful young girl appeared to him in a dream. She seemed so real that he stretched out his arm to touch her and, as he did so, the vision melted away. The maiden's face remained clear in his mind, however, and, throughout the next day, he could not banish her from his thoughts.

On the following night, the maiden returned to his dreams. This time, she brought a tiny harp with her, and she sang him the sweetest songs he had ever heard. Oenghus rested well that night but, as dawn began to break, the girl vanished again and his heart was heavy. No food passed his lips that day and his spirit was troubled with thoughts of her.

This train of events continued, night after night, for a whole year. Throughout this time, Oenghus pined for the maid and his people became concerned for him. Physicians were summoned, but they could not put a name to his sickness or discover any cure for it. Eventually, Fergne, the most famous of the healers, was brought to see him. At once, Fergne recognized that the ailment lay in

Oenghus's mind, not his body. Taking him to one side, he told him of his finding: 'I think that it is for the love of some beautiful woman that you are wasting away like this.'

'That is true,' replied Oenghus. 'I see that my sickness has betrayed me.' Whereupon, he confessed all to Fergne, telling him of the enchanting maid who came each night to haunt his dreams.

The physician explained these things to Boann, the mother of Oenghus, and she sent her people to search through all of Ireland for the girl. For a whole year, they hunted in every corner of the land; on remote mountain-tops, in the darkest depths of the forest, and in the meanest of dwelling-places. At the end of all this time they had still found no sign of her. Meanwhile, Oenghus continued to waste away.

Then Fergne made another suggestion. 'Send to Bodb, in his fairy-dwelling in Munster. He is the king of all the Sidhe and no knowledge can be hidden from him.'

This was done. Bodb agreed to do whatever lay within his power to find the girl. He proved as good as his word. At the end of the year, messengers arrived to say that the maid had been discovered at Lough Beul Draguin, at the Harp of Cliach.

Oenghus sped to the place as if he had wings on his feet. There, at the water's edge, he spied thrice fifty maidens and, among them, the girl that he had sought for three long years. The maidens were linked in pairs with silver

chains. Alone among them all, the beautiful girl from the dream had her own necklet, made of burnished gold.

'Do you know her name?' asked Oenghus.

'Certainly,' replied Bodb, 'she is Caer, the daughter of Ethal Anbual, from the fairy-dwelling of Uaman in Connacht. But you may not speak with her now. First, you must ask the permission of Medb and Ailill, the King of Connacht, for it is in their territory that she lives.'

So the Dagda took his son, Oenghus, and they went together to see Medb and Ailill at Cruachan. There, they were made welcome and a great feast was laid before them. The festivities lasted for a week until, at last, Ailill asked the Dagda the reason for his journey. The latter then gave a full account of his son's wasting sickness and asked if the girl could be given to him.

'We have no power over her,' said Medb, 'but we will send for her father and it may be that he will look kindly on your request.'

So, messengers were sent with all speed to fetch Ethal Anbual, but he refused to come, knowing the purpose that lay behind the summons. 'Let it be known,' he told the messengers, 'that I will not give my daughter to the son of the Dagda.'

Medb and Ailill were furious when they heard this insolent reply. Immediately, they sent a troop of their fiercest warriors to mete out a violent retribution. Within three days, the dwelling-place of Ethal Anbual had been levelled to the ground and he himself was brought in chains before them.

'I command you now,' boomed Ailill, 'deliver your daughter to the son of the Dagda.'

'I fear, lord, I cannot,' the wretched man complained. 'There is a power over her and her maidens that far exceeds my authority.'

'What power is this?' Ailill demanded.

'It is an enchantment. Caer and her maidens must reside in the shape of birds for one year, and in their own form throughout the year that follows. Go seek her next summer at Lough Beul Draguin, and you will see if I am telling the truth.' The sincerity of his words was apparent to all and the chains were struck from his wrists.

Oenghus waited with impatience for the arrival of summer, hardly daring to believe that his long search might be drawing to a close. When the time came, he hurried to the lough and watched in wonder as thrice fifty swans coasted on the water. Each had a silver chain, save only one, which was adorned with a circlet of shining gold. Oenghus called out to her, 'Caer, come over and speak with me, I implore you.'

'Who is it that summons me thus?' she cried.

'It is I, Oenghus. Please come and talk with me,' he urged.

'Only if you promise that I may return to the water, if I wish,' Caer replied.

'I swear it,' he vowed.

On hearing this assurance, the maid swam over and laid her downy head in Oenghus's lap. Then, to show her that he would keep true to his oath, he turned himself into the shape of a swan. Together, they glided into the lough and swam round it three times. After that, they spread their wings and rose up from the water, flying in that shape all the way to the Dagda's palace at Brug na Bóinne. And, as they flew, their voices made a honeyed sound that was so sweet to the ea, that all who heard it were lulled into a sleep which lasted for the space of three days and three nights.

Caer stayed with Oenghus ever afterwards. And, for the favours they had shown him, Oenghus held a great bond of friendship with Medb and Ailill. It was because of this that he offered them assistance, during the great cattle raid of Cooley.

The Wooing of Etain

MIDIR AND ETAIN

It happened once that Midir came at Samhain time to Brug na Bóinne, to visit Oenghus his foster-son. Together, they sat upon the mound, watching the young men of the land playing before them. Soon, a quarrel broke out among some of the boys and Midir rose from his place, to make peace between them. But it took him some time to quell the fighting and, in the process, he suffered a painful injury. A dart of holly leaves speared into him, putting out one of his eyes. Ruefully, Midir walked back to Oenghus, carrying his eye in his hand.

'Would that I had never paid this call on you,' he cried, 'for now I am both shamed and disfigured. Nevermore can I return to my home at Brí Leith, with such a blemish on my face.'

'Fear not,' said Oenghus soothingly, 'for I will seek a means to cure you.' True to his word, he instantly despatched messengers to fetch Dian Cécht, the great healer. In all of Ireland, none could surpass his skills. He it was who had tended Nuada after the great battle of Magh Tuireadh, supplying him with a silver hand to replace the one lost in the fray.

Swiftly, Dian Cécht was brought to the palace at Brug na Bóinne, where he tended Midir until his wound was fully healed. Oenghus rejoiced at his foster-father's recovery and bade him accept his hospitality until the end of the year, to complete his convalescence in comfort.

Now Midir showed his pride. 'I will not stay here with you,' he replied, 'unless I have some reward for my injury.'

'What kind of reward do you seek?' asked Oenghus.

'That is easily told,' said Midir. 'Bring me a chariot worth seven slave-girls, apparel that is fitting for my rank, and the hand of the fairest maiden in Ireland.'

'I have the chariot and the clothing,' mused Oenghus, 'but I am at a loss to name a woman of such quality.'

'I will tell you then,' said Midir. 'I know of none fairer than Etain, daughter of Ailill, the king of the Ulstermen.'

This was all the prompting Oenghus needed. Straight away, he set off for Ulster, where he announced his purpose to Ailill. The latter was reluctant to part with his daughter, however, and exacted a high price from the Dagda's son. Twelve plains were to be cleared of all their waste and scrub, so that Ailill's people could make dwellings there and graze their cattle upon the land. The task was a mighty one, but Oenghus went directly to his father and enlisted his aid. In the space of a single night, the Dagda managed to clear each of the twelve sites, from the plain of Macha to the plain of Muirthemne.

Oenghus returned to Ulster to claim his prize, but Ailill was not yet satisfied. Next, he demanded that the soil in these twelve plains should be cut and shaped, so that the waters from twelve marshes would become rivers, full and swollen, which would irrigate the land for his people. Once again, Oenghus turned to his father for help and, during the following night, the Dagda performed a second miraculous feat, carving twelve new waterways into Ailill's land.

Next day, Oenghus came once more before the Ulster king. 'You have shown great generosity towards my people,' declared Ailill. 'Now I must have my portion. Give me the maid's weight in gold and silver and she is yours.'

Oenghus nodded in agreement. 'Bring her forth and let it be done.' Etain was summoned into the chamber and the deal was swiftly concluded. This done, Oenghus returned home with her to Brug na Bóinne.

Midir was delighted with his new bride and,

true to his word, remained with his foster-son until the end of the year. Then he travelled back to Brí Leith, to rejoin his household. Most of Midir's people were overjoyed at seeing him again, after so long an absence. There was, however, one dissenter. For Midir had another wife, a bold and cunning woman named Fuamnach, and she was filled with jealousy at the arrival of the newcomer.

Fuamnach had been reared by Bresal the Druid, who was well versed in enchantments and spells. So, while Midir fawned over Etain, taking great pleasure in showing her the richness of his lands and the wonders of his treasure-house, Fuamnach stole away to see her foster-father. Bresal counselled her wisely, urging her to conceal her displeasure from Etain, until the time was ripe for revenge. He also gave her the means of carrying it out, by teaching her the subtle art of transformation.

Eagerly, Fuamnach returned to Brí Leith and awaited her chance. This was not long in coming. One day, while Midir was out hunting with his people, the two women were left alone in the palace. When Etain came into her chamber, Fuamnach rose from her seat and offered it to her rival. 'You are taking the place of a good woman,' she said angrily, as Etain sat down. Then, taking up a scarlet wand fashioned from the bough of a rowan tree, she struck the Ulster princess on the shoulder. Now, the dark teachings of Bresal came into force. A look of panic spread across Etain's face and then no look at all, as her form dissolved into the air. In her place, all that remained was a pool of water. Fuamnach gazed down at this approvingly and then went off to Bresal's house. When Midir returned home later that day, he discovered that both his wives had vanished without trace.

But Fuamnach's spell had not yet run its course. Etain was not trapped for long in her watery prison. In the humid atmosphere of Brí Leith, she soon began to change again, this time assuming the form of a purple fly. Despite its lowly state, there was nothing ordinary about this fly. Its head was as large and pleasant to behold as that of the noblest courtier; its wings beat with a sound more delicate than the finest harp-string; and its breath was as fragrant as a meadow full of flowers. Its merest touch could dispel any sickness and sate the hunger pangs of a starving man.

Midir was aware that this wondrous creature was Etain and allowed it to accompany him on his travels. The noise of its buzzing inspired him as he went about his royal business, soothed him when he slept, and woke him whenever one of his enemies came near. As long as it remained by his side, Midir felt no desire to take another wife.

When Fuamnach learned of the favour shown to the purple fly, she was consumed with jealousy. Using another of Bresal the Druid's spells, she turned herself into a raging wind which swept through Midir's palace and carried Etain away. For many long years, the fly was cast about and buffeted by this wind, unable to alight on any surface. Through all the provinces of Ireland it was blown, through marshes and bogs, along rocky coasts and inlets, until it finally came to rest on the edge of Oenghus's cloak.

'Welcome fair Etain,' he said, gathering up the exhausted creature. 'Much effort did it cost me to win you for Midir, but I see that it has profited you little. Unhappy woman, torn from the bosom of her home; unhappy husband, deprived of his lovely wife.' So he gave the purple fly shelter, allowing it to nestle in the folds of his cloak. Whenever his wanderings took him away from Brug na Bóinne, he carried it at his breast, and whenever he was in the fairy mound, he placed it in a pleasant bower, filled with scented herbs and flowers. In this way, Etain recovered her strength, regaining all the charms that had so delighted Midir.

Eventually, Fuamnach came to hear of her rival's good fortune and resolved to bring her new torments. Once more she turned into a howling wind that ripped the fly away from Oenghus's protection. For another lengthy span of years, it became a plaything of the elements, tossed about by the force of the enchanted storm and hurled along every corner of Ireland's shores.

Oenghus, meanwhile, was enraged at the treatment meted out to one in his care. Immediately, he took up arms and searched for Fuamnach's trail. Within days, he tracked her down at Oenach Bodbgnai, in the house of Bresal the Druid. There, he beheaded her and attached her skull, still dripping with gore, to the side of his chariot. Then he drove back to Brug na Bóinne, with the trophy dangling by his side.

For weary Etain, it seemed as if an eternity of suffering followed, before she reached her next resting place. This time, she settled on the roof of a house in Ulster, where Etar the Warrior was feasting with his companions. A final gust propelled the fly through the roof and into a golden goblet on the banqueting table. The vessel was full of milk and, as the insect struggled to reach the surface, Etar's wife picked up the goblet and drained it, swallowing Etain along with the liquid. The woman then bore her for the next nine months, before giving birth to her as an earthly maid and naming her Etain. And the time between her first begetting, as the daughter of Ailill, and her second birth was one thousand and twelve years.

Etain was brought up in the household of Etar at Inber Cichmaine. There, she was surrounded by fifty maidens, the daughters of the neighbouring chieftains, whom Etar reared as her companions. And upon a certain day, when all these maids were gathered at the riverside to bathe, they saw a horseman riding towards them from the plain. His mount was golden brown, with a fleecy mane and a light, prancing step. About his shoulders, he wore a stunning cloak of emerald green, fastened with a brooch of burnished gold. In his right hand, he carried a five-pronged spear with a shaft of beaten gold while, slung across his back, there was a silver shield with a horn-shaped boss. When he drew near, the youth climbed down from his magnificent horse and stared at the maidens gathered before him. They, for their part, gazed at his flaxen locks, tumbling down over his brow, and were instantly filled with love for him.

After a brief pause, he spoke: 'I bring you greetings, Etain, you who are here today with this fair company. You are the one who healed a monarch's eye; you are the one swallowed up in a cup of gold. For your sake, a king will chase the birds of Teffa and let his coursers drown in the dark waters of Lake Dá Airbrech. For your sake, a bloody war will be waged in Meath. Many of the Sidhe will be destroyed and thousands of brave Eochaid's soldiers will meet their doom. So, greetings, Etain. A malicious spirit brought you here and, in your wake, you will leave a trail of heartbreak and despair.'

After this chilling message, the young warrior climbed back on his horse and turned away from the maidens. And none of them knew where he had come from, nor where he was going.

AILILL'S SICK-BED

There was once a noble lord called Eochaid Airem, who gained the high kingship of all Ireland. The chieftains of the five provinces were obedient to him, and he held sway over a network of powerful strongholds. Among these, none was more pleasing to him than the fort of Frémain in Tethba.

After reigning for a year, Eochaid summoned all of Ireland's worthies to attend him at the Festival of Tara, in order to assess the tributes and taxes that were to be levied over the coming five years. But Eochaid's subjects refused. For, as they pointed out, no king could preside over the Festival unless he had a wife that was his equal in rank and bearing. Eochaid, for all his virtues, had no queen.

The Sidhe

F EW THINGS CONJURE up the mystery and romance of early Irish legends as vividly as the Sidhe. These were the fairy mounds or dwellings, where the ancient gods were thought to reside. Fairies, in this context, should not be envisaged as the cute, winged creatures that appear in later children's literature. They were the shadowy figures of older, supernatural beings, and their influence on the world of mortals was highly unpredictable. Some were helpful to Ireland's heroes, while others were driven by pure malice.

Much of the lore about the Sidhe derived from a series of stories about the island's earliest inhabitants. According to these tales, ancient Ireland was ruled by five successive waves of invaders: the Partholónians, the Nemedians, the Firbolg, the Tuatha Dé Danaan and the

The Mound of the Hostages, Tara, County Meath
In the legends, Tara was the home of gods as well as the stronghold of the high kings. The name comes from Niall of the Nine Hostages, who ruled at Tara in the fifth century.

Milesians. It was the fourth of these groups which figured most prominently in the early myths. Their name can be translated as 'the People of Danu', the latter being a goddess of fertility, who is best remembered as the mother of the Dagda.

The Tuatha Dé Danaan won great victories over the Firbolg and a band of sea pirates called the Fomorians, but they eventually met defeat at the hands of a quasi-historical people, the Milesians. This marked the end of the Danaans' rule, but not their influence. Using the vestiges of their magical powers, they spread a veil of invisibility over themselves, so that they could appear or disappear at will. At this point, the Dagda allotted a Sidh to each of his people, before resigning his leadership over them. This is the situation outlined at the start of *The Fate of the Children of Lir*.

ENCHANTED DWELLINGS

After this, the Danaans retired to their Sidhe, where they were no longer visible to the eyes of men. From the outside, all that could be seen were grassy mounds and the ruins of ancient fortresses. Inside, however, the gods lived a life of ease and luxury. There were endless supplies of ale and meat, served up in cauldrons which never ran dry, and most of the time was spent in feasting and revelry. Better still, the Danaans did not suffer from sickness, pain or the horrors of old age. Even so, the gods did not remain permanently cloistered inside their fairy palaces, but ventured out to interfere in the affairs of mortals. Inevitably, encounters of this kind provided the dynamics for many of the early Irish legends. By the same token, human access to the Sidhe was sometimes possible at Samhain, that magical period when the boundaries between the real world and the Otherworld were broken down.

The description of the Sidhe as mounds has fuelled speculation that the idea was inspired by Ireland's prehistoric burial mounds. Certainly, archaeological evidence has confirmed that many of the major sites – which were constructed long before the Celtic period – were known to later generations and were used for a variety of ritual activities. It is significant, too, that Ireland's most celebrated ancient monument, the megalithic complex at Newgrange, was identified in the legends as the grandest of the Sidhe. This was the home of the Dagda, the father of the gods. Here, according to tradition, there were three trees, which bore fruit all year round; here, too, was the oven made by Druimne, which consisted of thrice nine spits and thrice nine cauldrons, warmed by the heat of a flame which rose to the ceiling of the chamber, and which produced an inexhaustible supply of food.

WOMEN OF THE SIDHE

Some aspects of the Sidhe were absorbed into later folk traditions. The most notable of these was the banshee, which takes its name from *bean sidhe* (woman of the Sidhe). Banshees became attached to specific tribes or clans and used to leave their Sidhe, in order to warn family members of impending doom. In more recent times, this warning was delivered in the form of an unearthly shriek or howl, usually heard within the precincts of the ancestral home. In earlier myths, however, the banshee was frequently equated with the Washer at the Ford. Many of the heroes in the Ulster cycle met this ominous fairy woman shortly before their death, washing their bloodstained garments or armour in the waters of a stream.

Entrance stone, Newgrange
The graves at Newgrange were known to early storytellers as Brug na Bóinne (Palace of the Boyne), the home of the Dagda.

The king acknowledged the problem and sent out messengers, to scour the land for a suitable bride. These messengers came from every section of his household. There were horsemen from his private guard, learned wizards and counsellors, and warriors stationed on the marches of his lands. These royal officers were to search Ireland north and south, from coast to coast, until they found him a suitable mate. One condition alone did he make: that the woman in question should have had no other husband before him.

Time passed and the messengers returned with their choice. With one accord, they named Etain, daughter of Etar, as the fairest maid in the kingdom. Eochaid listened to their descriptions of her fine looks and gracious manners, before deciding to travel down to Inber Cichmaine to see the girl for himself. He came upon her some way from the palace, bathing at a secluded spring. At once, her beauty eclipsed all the accounts that he had heard. Her skin was as pale as the snow of a single night, while her cheeks had the tint of a budding rose. Her golden hair was plaited into four strands, each adorned with a tiny golden sphere. Eochaid watched as she shook the plaits loose and combed them out with a silver brush. Her tunic was made of green silk embroidered with golden stitching and, about it, she wore a purple mantle, fastened with a gleaming metal brooch in the shape of a bird.

Eochaid was transfixed. Immediately, he sent ahead to Etar, to discover the girl's bride-price and whether or not she had ever been wed. Once these matters had been satisfactorily arranged, he returned with her to Tara, where she was welcomed by his people with much rejoicing.

Now Eochaid had two brothers, Eochaid Fedlech and Ailill Anglonnach. The latter was soon to be better known by the nickname 'Ailill of the Single Stain', for his character was stained by the love that he bore for his new sister-in-law. This passion afflicted him from the moment he first set eyes upon Etain, during the wedding celebrations at the Festival of Tara. Throughout the month-long feast, which ran from the fourteen days preceding Samhain to the fourteen days which followed,

Ailill could scarcely tear his gaze away from the girl. These attentions did not go unnoticed. At one point, Ailill's wife, the daughter of Luchta of the Red Hand, turned to him and chided: 'Why do you look so fondly on your brother's wife? Your stares might easily be seen as a token of love for her.' This made Ailill ashamed and he resolved to look upon Etain no more.

After the festival was over, the men of Ireland returned to their homes. Ailill struggled with his conscience, but his feelings for Etain only grew stronger. Such was their potency that he eventually fell ill, taking to his bed with a wasting sickness. Eochaid was much concerned over his brother's mysterious condition and had him conveyed to the stronghold of Frémain, hoping that the beauteous prospect from this spot might help to restore his kinsman to health.

But Ailill grew steadily worse, barely eating and sleeping. So Eochaid called upon Fachtna, his personal physician, and bade him tend to his brother. Obediently, Fachtna examined the stricken man and laid a hand upon his chest. At this, Ailill uttered a deep, forlorn sigh. Fachtna then removed his hand and gave his judgment.

'There are but two causes for such an ailment as this,' he said knowingly. 'Only the pangs of love or the fire of jealousy can produce such suffering. Which of these is troubling you, my son?' But Ailill was ashamed and refused to answer, lest he bring dishonour upon himself and his family. So the physician left the room, and the cause of Ailill's pining remained a secret.

After a time, Eochaid was obliged to travel forth from Frémain, to make a royal progress around his kingdom. It hurt him sorely to do so, for he felt sure that his brother would die during his absence. Accordingly, he went to Etain and charged her with his care. 'Lady,' he said, 'deal gently with my brother. Do everything within your power to keep him alive.' Then he paused for a moment, scarcely willing to continue with his instructions:

'And if he should die, see that he is buried with full pomp and honour. Let a pillar-stone be raised upon his grave, and have his name carved upon it in letters of ogham.' Then the king embarked on his year-long journey, convinced that he would see Ailill no more.

In the weeks that followed, Etain fulfilled her husband's wishes dutifully. Every day, she went to Ailill's chamber, to mop his brow and coax him to eat. After a while, it became clear to her that his condition seemed to improve upon her arrival and then deteriorated when she was about to depart. Puzzled, she decided to question Ailill about this. 'Have you no idea what it is that ails you?' she asked. 'You must be aware that we would do anything in our power to help you.'

Ailill hesitated before answering. 'Lady,' he confessed, 'it is love that causes me to sicken thus.'

'Tell me the maid's name,' said Etain quickly. 'If she is one of my serving women, I will have her brought to your side, to ease your sickness.'

'Alas,' said Ailill slowly, 'she is none of these. The woman I love is my brother's wife.'

Etain was silent, numbed by the revelation.

'My passion arose more than a year ago,' he continued, 'and I have been in thrall to it ever since. It grips me more tightly than my skin. It rules over me more powerfully than anger or strength of arms. Loftier than the highest star can it reach and, such is its force, that it could tear the four corners of the earth asunder.'

Etain went away and considered this. It grieved her to witness Ailill's despair and she made up her mind to help him. Next day, she returned to his chamber. 'It is a pity that you did not tell me earlier of the root of your sickness,' she chided gently, 'for I am pledged to do all within my power to cure you. Even so, the king must not be shamed inside his own house. So, meet with me tomorrow upon the hill that lies beyond this stronghold. There, at break of day, you shall have my embraces.'

Throughout that afternoon, Ailill waited with impatience for the hours to pass. Then night came and he could not sleep. During the hours of darkness, his eyes remained wide open. Finally, when the trysting time arrived, he fell into a deep and heavy sleep.

Etain, meanwhile, went to the hill at the appointed time. As dawn broke, she saw a man walking towards her. He appeared exactly like Ailill and he had the gait of a weak and ailing man, just risen from his sick-bed. Etain addressed him, and both the sound of his voice and the words that he spoke were precisely what she expected from the king's brother.

The queen returned to Ailill's chamber at the third hour of the day, just as he awoke from his slumbers. He looked pained and sheepish, and Etain quizzed him on his behaviour.

'My lord, you look sorrowful. What is it that troubles you?'

'I am full of shame,' he replied, 'for I slept right through our trysting time and never went to meet with you. Now I will never be healed.'

'Do not concern yourself,' said Etain, 'for tomorrow is another day. Meet me on the hill at the time we agreed, and I shall cure you of all your ills.'

That night, Ailill resolved to stay wide awake, to avoid any repetition of the problem. He had a great fire lit in his hearth, so that the room was as bright as a summer day. In addition, he had a basin of ice-cold water placed beside his bed, so that he could splash his face whenever he felt drowsy. Hour after hour he lay awake, waiting for the dawn. But, as the time approached, he felt a deep, unnatural tiredness overcoming him. When the first rays of light broke through the sky, he was fast asleep.

Outside, on the hill, the same stranger kept the rendezvous with Etain. As before, he seemed identical to Ailill, both in his manner and his appearance, and the queen had no reason to doubt him. When she returned to his chamber, however, she discovered that the same deception had been practised upon her. Once more, she consoled Ailill over his disappointment and agreed to meet with him on the morrow. Secretly, though, she was convinced that he was under some enchantment and that, for all his good intentions, he would never leave his bed.

Even so, Etain kept her tryst on the third day and, sure enough, as dawn broke, she saw the same figure climbing up the hill towards her. The stranger smiled at her but, this time, Etain was determined to challenge him.

'You are not the one that I am due to meet,' she said. 'Who are you and what is your purpose? For my part, I must tell you that I have not come here with any wanton or unlawful intent. My only desire is to cure a man, who is sick with love for me.'

'In that case, it would be more fitting if you trysted with me,' replied the other, 'for when you were a princess of Ulster, the daughter of King Ailill, I was your husband.'

'How can this be?' asked Etain, astonished. 'For I do not even know your name.'

'I am called Midir of Brí Leith and, when we were wed, a mighty bride-price was paid on your account,' he replied. 'Twelve plains were cleared and twelve rivers cut into the land. More than this, your father received your weight in gold and silver.'

'If that is so, then what strange accident could have been driven us apart and caused me to lose all memory of you?' Etain exclaimed in disbelief.

'No natural event, it is true,' admitted Midir. 'It was the spells of Bresal the Druid and the sorcery of his charge, Fuamnach, which created the rift between us. But all things can be mended. Come with me now and we shall be the happy couple that once we were.'

'Not so,' declared Etain. 'It may be that you tell the truth, but I will not exchange the high king of all Ireland for the like of you; a stranger whose position and parentage are unknown to me.'

Despite this, Midir continued to plead his cause. 'Do not reject me so lightly, fair Etain. Our fortunes are linked more closely than you suppose, for it was I who caused the king's brother to fall in love with you and I, too, who prevented him from coming to your trysts, so that your honour might be spared.'

Still Etain remained unmoved, determined to stay with Eochaid at Frémain. At last, Midir bowed his head, seeing that she would not be swayed.

'One last question,' he begged, 'and then I will take my leave.'

'Name it,' said Etain.

'Would you come with me, if Eochaid gave his permission?'

Etain looked him straight in the eye. 'I would,' she replied.

'Then that must satisfy me,' said Midir and a moment later he was gone.

Now Etain returned to the stronghold, where she found Ailill looking much brighter. Both his sickness and his desire were completely spent. So she told him of her meeting with Midir and he appeared greatly pleased. 'Thanks be to the gods. This matter has turned out well for both of us. I am cured forever and your honour has been preserved.'

Ailill's delight was matched by that of Eochaid, upon his return. He was overjoyed to find his brother still alive and praised Etain to the skies, when he heard of all that she had done for him. 'Surely,' he thought, 'no man can be more fortunate than I; to have such a wife and to know that she will always be by my side.'

THE RETURN OF MIDIR

One beautiful summer morning, Eochaid Airem rose early from his bed and went to gaze out over his land. He climbed up to the highest point of Tara and admired the view. Before him stretched the fair plain of Breg, a sea of colour with its flowers and blooms of every hue.

Eochaid fancied that he was all alone but, as he looked around, he noticed that a stranger was making his way towards him. The fellow appeared to be a warrior, for he carried a five-pointed spear in one hand and a silver shield studded with sparkling gems in the other. His shoulder-length hair was golden, his eyes were grey and twinkling, and his tunic was made of the finest purple cloth. He seemed friendly enough, but Eochaid was wary, for no such man had been present in Tara on the previous evening and the entrance gates to the high enclosure had not yet been opened.

The stranger came closer and placed himself under Eochaid's protection. This was granted. 'I bid you welcome, brave warrior,' said the king, 'though I must confess that I do not recognize you.'

'I expected no less gracious a greeting,' replied the stranger.

'How can that be,' enquired the king, 'for I am sure that we have never met?'

'You may not recognize me, my lord, but I know you,' the stranger asserted.

'Pray then,' said Eochaid, 'tell me your name.'

'It is not a name of great renown,' the other admitted. 'I am called Midir of Brí Leith.'

'And what is it that brings you to my realm, Midir?' asked Eochaid.

'I have come to challenge you to a game of chess, my lord,' replied Midir.

This answer surprised the king, though it also pleased him, for he was justly proud of his skill at the game. 'I would happily oblige you,' said Eochaid, 'though I cannot do so at present. I keep my set in the queen's chamber and she will still be sleeping at this hour.'

'No matter,' said Midir. 'I have brought my own set with me and it is just as fine as yours.'

Indeed, this was no less than the truth, for the board was made of silver and the pieces were solid gold. As Midir laid them out, bright jewels gleamed at every corner of the chessboard and even the bag which held the chessmen was wrought from shining golden threads.

Midir offered Eochaid his choice of colours, but the latter would not play until they had named a stake. 'It shall be as you ask,' replied the challenger. 'What would you like to play for?'

Eochaid shrugged his shoulders. 'I don't mind. You choose.'

'If you win,' Midir proposed, 'I shall give you fifty fiery steeds. They will be dappled grey, but with blood-red heads, flaring nostrils and hooves that run like the wind. I will deliver them by the third hour of tomorrow morning.'

Eochaid agreed and offered a similar stake. Then the two men started to play. From the start, it seemed that their skills were evenly matched, for the game was long and hard. The sun was high in the sky, before it reached its conclusion. At last, however, Eochaid triumphed. Then Midir stood up and congratulated his opponent, promising to return on the following morning with his prize.

Next day, Eochaid rose at dawn and went out once more to the high place of Tara. It was not long before he saw Midir coming towards him, leading the fifty dapple-grey horses. At first, Eochaid was taken aback, for he had not heard Midir arrive and he knew that the gates to the enclosure should still be closed. Even so, his surprise was soon overtaken by delight, for the horses were even sleeker and finer than he had imagined. What was more, each of them was fitted out with a fine bridle of enamelled bronze.

'Welcome, friend,' said Eochaid, 'I see you are as honourable as your word.'

'Whatever is promised must be paid,' replied Midir. 'Shall we play again?'

'Willingly,' agreed Eochaid. 'What shall our stake be this time?'

'If you win,' said Midir, 'I shall bring you fifty dark-skinned boars, fattened and ready for the pot,

with the sweetest meat that you ever tasted. In addition, I will give you a huge cauldron to cook them in.'

Eochaid nodded and Midir set out the board. Then the two men began their game and, for the next few hours, there was silence between them. Eventually, Eochaid won again and Midir took his leave, promising to return with the boars.

After this, Eochaid went back down into Tara and showed off his new horses to his kinsmen. Most were impressed, but Eochaid's foster-father took him aside and counselled prudence. 'This is a man of great power, who has come against you, my son. Make sure that you set him difficult tasks, and guard against wagers which you cannot pay.'

Eochaid took this advice and, in subsequent meetings with Midir, he did not play for riches, but for services that would benefit his people. Midir was asked to clear away the rocks and boulders from the plain of Meath, so that his farmers could work the land; he was charged with removing the reeds and rushes from the marshy land around the stronghold of Frémain; and he was told to build a causeway across the bog of Lamrach, so that Eochaid's people could pass freely over it.

Midir performed all these tasks without demur. Workers were brought from Brí Leith and these laboured night and day, to fulfil the promises that their lord had made. Eochaid went out onto the land to watch them, and he noticed that the men of the Sidhe harnessed their oxen across the shoulder rather than the forehead, to gain more purchase. Immediately, he gave orders that his people were to do likewise, and this is how he

gained the name of Eochaid Airem or Eochaid the Ploughman, for this was the first time that the oxen of Ireland had been harnessed in this manner.

When all these labours had been performed, Midir came once more to Tara. 'What stake shall we play for today?' enquired Eochaid, confident that he had the measure of his man.

'Let the winner determine that, when the game is over,' said Midir.

'Agreed,' said Eochaid and the two men began their next game. This time, Midir triumphed.

'You have won your wager,' said Eochaid, rising to his feet.

'I could have won it long ago, had I so wished,' replied Midir.

'Then what do you desire?' enquired the king.

'Grant me that I may hold Etain in my arms and obtain a kiss from her,' came the reply.

Eochaid was silent for a while, before nodding his agreement. 'Come again one month from today,' he said, 'and you shall have what you ask.'

Then Midir departed, and he did not come again to Tara until a month had elapsed. On the appointed day, he returned and made his way into the great banqueting hall. Eochaid and Etain were there, in the very heart of the palace, and around them were gathered all the fighting men of Ireland. For now, at this late hour, Eochaid was mindful of the warnings of his foster-father and he feared that Midir might come with a great host, to carry away the queen. Accordingly, he ringed the walls of Tara with his finest champions, and gave orders that the gates and doors of the palace were to be made fast.

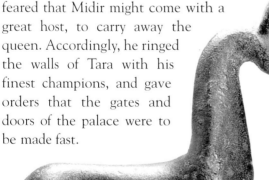

But Midir came alone and unannounced. He strode into the hall, just as Etain was pouring out wine for the king and his companions. His appearance caused astonishment and a deathly hush fell upon the assembled feasters.

'I have come to claim my prize,' stated Midir. 'I carried out all the pledges that were due to you, Eochaid, and now it is my turn. Whatever was promised must be paid.'

'I have not yet made my mind up about that,' responded the king cautiously.

'You gave your word,' said Midir firmly. 'You have yielded up Etain to me, for of what else does love consist if not of embraces and kisses.'

Etain blushed deeply when she heard these words, but Midir reassured her: 'Be not ashamed, my lady, for you have done nothing amiss. I offered you treasures and riches when we met upon the hill, but you refused me aught unless Eochaid allowed it. The fact that I have won you now is not of your doing.'

'It is true,' admitted Etain, 'that I promised to go with you, if the king gave his permission ...'

'But I do not permit it,' interrupted Eochaid, 'though he may take you in his arms in the centre of this chamber. That was the extent of my promise.'

'So be it,' said Midir, leading Etain away from her husband. Then, in the blink of an eye, he took his sword in his left hand and slipped his right arm around the lady's waist. Effortlessly, he bore her up, carrying her out through the skylight and into the evening air. Eochaid's men rushed at them, but they were much too slow. Then they hastened outside, but all they could see were two swans, linked by a golden chain, flying gracefully away from Tara.

Consumed with anger, Eochaid immediately assembled an army to try and recapture his lost wife. Their first assault was on the fairy mound of Femun, for it was in this direction that the swans had headed. Eochaid's men dug up the mound and did battle with the inhabitants, but they found no trace of Etain.

But this did not deter the attackers. With vengeance in his heart, Eochaid swore that he would destroy every Sidh in Ireland, if this was the only way to recover his beloved. He was as good as his word. For years on end, the high king's men laid siege to all the fairy dwellings that they came across on their search, and much blood was shed on either side.

At last, Eochaid's army came to Brí Leith, where Midir and Etain had made their home. Long and hard was the struggle for this fairy mound – some men say that the fighting continued for nine full years. Finally, when the walls of the mound were close to collapse, Midir appeared before Eochaid.

'Lay down your arms,' he demanded, 'and I will restore the queen to you, even though she is rightfully mine.'

Eochaid agreed and commanded his soldiers to withdraw from the mound. Then, next morning, he beheld a miraculous sight. At the third hour of the morning, a group of fifty women walked towards his camp, every one of them bearing the form and features of Etain.

'Choose your wife now,' commanded Midir, 'and she shall return home with you. If you fail to find her, then she is lost to you forever.'

Eochaid's men marvelled at this spectacle, and debated how their lord might make his choice. The king, however, had no such doubts. 'Let vessels of wine be brought forth,' he ordered, 'for in all of Tara, there is none who can pour wine like Etain. That is how I shall know her.'

As he commanded, so was it done. The wine was fetched and, as Eochaid watched, each maid in turn poured out a measure from the flagon. One by one, he rejected them all, until only two were left. Then, as the first of these raised her vessel, the king made up his mind. 'This is Etain,' he said, 'even though she is not serving in her usual manner.'

So saying, he bore the woman away with him in triumph and returned to Tara. And the men of Ireland rejoiced, seeing their king finally reunited with his beloved queen.

A little while later, Midir appeared once more before Eochaid. 'Are you content with your choice?' he enquired of the king.

'I am,' replied Eochaid.

'So am I,' said Midir, 'for I must tell you that the woman that you picked is not your wife. Etain was with child when I raised her out of Tara and, in the fullness of time, she gave birth to a daughter. She is with you now, while Etain resides with me. You have lost your wife once more, this time forever.' With these words, Midir disappeared, leaving Eochaid to his despair.

The Punishment of the Children of Tuireann

THE DEATH OF CIAN

In the days when the Tuatha Dé Danaan ruled over Ireland, the country was oppressed by Fomorian raiders. They forced every man to pay a tribute of an ounce of gold, on pain of having his nose smitten from his face. This tribute was paid for many years, until the coming of Lugh of the Long Arms. No warrior was ever better equipped than he. He rode the steed of Manannán Mac Lir, Enbarr of the Flowing Mane, which ran so swiftly that no adversary could catch it; he wore Manannán's breast-plate, which no weapon could ever pierce; and he wielded a great sword, the Answerer, which cut through flesh like butter, creating wounds that no healer could hope to cure.

Lugh came against the Fomorian tax-gatherers in all his might and scattered them like cattle. Nine alone survived, to bear the story of his deeds back to the Fomorian people.

Animal Symbolism

THE SYMBOLIC IMPORTANCE of animals can be discerned in every aspect of Celtic life. Archaeological evidence has shown that a wide variety of creatures was used in sacrifices and in certain funerary rites. Pigs, cattle, horses, and even dogs were buried along with their owners, or else deposited in deep pit-shafts. Often, these bones were carefully arranged in order to emphasize their ritual significance. In addition, animal imagery was an ever-present feature in both the artworks and the literature of the Irish and their fellow-Celts.

LEGENDARY BEASTS

The bull, as might be guessed from its prominence in the *Táin*, was one of the most prestigious beasts. It was used as a symbol of power and wealth, and it figured in a number of sacred ceremonies. Chief among these was the *Tarbhfhess* or 'bull-sleep', through which the high kings of Ireland were selected. The event took place at Tara, where a bull was ritually slaughtered by a group of druids. One of their number feasted on the broth and the flesh of the animal, before being placed in a trance by his colleagues. While unconscious, he experienced a vision in which the identity of the next king was revealed. On the continent, the bull was usually revered as Tarvos Trigaranus, the 'bull with three cranes'. Images showing the beast with these birds have been found in a variety of Gaulish shrines, and the bull itself was sometimes depicted with three horns.

After the bull, the boar was the most potent animal symbol, with its dual references to war and the Otherworld. The strength and fierceness of the creature evoked obvious comparisons with warfare, and it was frequently portrayed on weapons and armour. On the Gundestrup Cauldron soldiers were shown carrying boar-headed war trumpets, while a shield found in the River Witham in England carries traces of a boar crest. There is evidence, too, that Celtic warriors used to adorn their helmets with tiny figurines of boars.

In the context of the afterlife, the flesh of the beast was the staple diet of slain heroes, while hapless hunters could be lured to the threshold of the Otherworld by magical boars.

Enchanted animals of this kind were commonplace in Celtic literature. The Welsh tale of Culhwch and Olwen, for example, was dominated by a lengthy quest for the evil king, who had been transformed into Twrch Trwyth, a monstrous boar. In the case of the gods, this type of shape-shifting was voluntary. The Morrigán, the most lethal of the Irish war goddesses, was often described in the epics as the battle-crow, on account of her taste for assuming this form, when appearing at battlefields to gloat over the dead and dying. The symbolism of her choice was obvious. Crows were traditionally associated with death, partly because of their colouring and

Terminal of an iron fire-dog
The horned bull was a strong Celtic icon that featured in many designs.

A Pictish symbol stone showing a salmon
The salmon was a symbol of knowledge and wisdom. It acquired these gifts by eating nuts from a magic tree.

partly because they fed on carrion. Humans, too, might be transformed, though this was usually as the result of a curse. Swans were another favourite guise for shape-shifters. Oenghus, for instance, fell in love with a maiden who had suffered this fate, while the children of Lir were doomed by their evil stepmother to spend 900 years as swans.

MAGICAL POWERS

Many animals were thought to possess special powers. Bronze figurines of dogs were sometimes left as offerings at Celtic healing shrines, as the saliva of a dog was thought to have curative properties. In the same way, the salmon was widely regarded as a source of wisdom. This is confirmed in a number of Irish and Welsh stories. Finn, the heroic leader of the Fenians, owed much of his success to the mental powers which he acquired after tasting the flesh of the Salmon of Knowledge in *The Boyhood of Finn*. Similarly, in one of the Welsh tales, a group of questing knights enlisted the aid of the Salmon of Llyn Llyw, to help them free a captive huntsman.

Horned creatures represented a broader range of attributes, such as majesty, virility and fertility. Finn's son, the warrior Oisin, was sometimes described as half-stag and half-man, because he was originally found abandoned, after his mother had been turned into a deer by the Black Druid. Celtic artists were also fond of portraying serpents with horns, presumably because the shedding and renewal of antlers was reminiscent of the way that snakes could slough their old skin. As a result, both deer and snakes were closely associated with Celtic fertility rites.

Now the Tuatha Dé Danaan were afraid, believing that the raiders would wreak a terrible vengeance on them. Undaunted, Lugh vowed that he would beat back any invasion force, and he asked King Bodb to give him warriors, to aid him in this task. But Bodb refused, fearing the wrath of the Fomorians. So Lugh called out for volunteers and, instantly, three men raised their hands. These were the sons of Cainte: Cian, Cu and Kethen.

'We will fight by your side,' they cried, 'and each of us will shield you from a hundred Fomorian warriors.' Lugh smiled, knowing that their boast was true, for Cian was his father.

Lugh's first command was to send this trio out into different parts of the countryside, to secure the aid of the people of the Sidhe. Thus it was that Cian came to be riding alone, across a plain to the north of Tara. Presently, he saw three armed horsemen heading towards him, whom he recognized as Brian, Iuchair and Iucharba, the three sons of Tuireann. Cian's heart sank at this, for there had long been enmity between the families of Cainte and Tuireann, and he felt sure that he would be killed. Concealment seemed his only option and, looking round, he noticed a herd of wild pigs. This gave him an idea. Taking out a golden, druidic wand, he changed himself into the shape of a pig and swiftly joined the herd.

But Cian had not been quick enough. 'Tell me,' said Brian, turning to his brothers. 'What do you think became of that warrior we saw in the distance?'

The others shrugged their shoulders, so Brian continued: 'No one could vanish like that by natural means. I fear there is some sorcery afoot here and, if the fellow is so keen to hide, you may be sure that he is no friend of ours.'

Unerringly, the trio made their way towards the pigs. 'The man is a fool,' said Brian, 'if he thinks that he can hide from us.' So saying, he took out his druid's rod and tapped his brothers on the shoulder. Immediately, they were transformed into a pair of sleek, swift-running hounds. Yelping eagerly, they rushed into the herd, hunting for the trail of the enchanted pig.

Cian saw that his luck was out and he left the herd, making a dash for a nearby thicket. But he could not outrun Brian's horse. In a moment, he was overtaken and the warrior hurled a spear at him, piercing him through the chest.

'You have done an evil deed,' moaned the beast, 'for you know very well that I am no animal.'

'I can hear that you have a human voice,' replied Brian, 'but I do not know who you are. Tell me your name.'

'I am Cian, son of Cainte, and I ask you now for mercy,' came the reply.

'That cannot be,' bellowed Brian, 'for there is bad blood between our families. I swear by the gods of the air that, if you had seven lives, I would take them from you seven times.'

'In that case,' said his stricken foe, 'allow me to return to my own shape before you kill me.'

'That will I grant,' agreed Brian, adding, 'for it is easier to kill a man than a pig.' Upon these words, Cian regained his form and stood defiantly before his attacker. Iuchair and Iucharba also resumed their normal shapes.

'Now have I fooled you, sons of Tuireann,' cried Cian, 'for, had you killed me as a beast, you would only have had to pay a trifling charge. If you kill me now, my son will demand an eric-fine, the full blood-price for killing a man.'

'Your son will never know,' said Brian, 'for we will not slay you with our swords, but with the rocks of the earth. That way, he will not realize that you have been killed by warriors.' So saying, the sons of Tuireann took up rocks and stones and hurled them at Cian, pelting him fiercely until his body was nothing more than a poor, disfigured mess.

They tried to bury him, to conceal the proof of the murder, but the earth would not receive such shame. Six times it cast the body up, leaving it above the ground. Only on the seventh time were the brothers able to cover it up with soil. Then they turned to leave. As they did so, a muffled voice came from below the earth. 'The blood you have spilled shall haunt you. It will follow your every step and doom shall be your reward.'

LUGH'S BLOOD-PRICE

Not long after the murder of Cian, Lugh did battle with the Fomorian raiders on the Great Plain of the Assembly. The contest was long and hard but, inspired by Lugh's example, the brave people of the Sidhe vanquished the Fomorians, putting their leaders to flight.

Towards the end of the day, Cu and Kethen rode over to Lugh to congratulate him, only to find that his brow was creased with worry. 'What ails you, lord?' Kethen cried out. 'Your victory is complete. The Fomorians will never trouble us again.'

'I fear for the safety of my father,' answered the great warrior. 'If he were alive, nothing could have prevented him from joining us here today, to lend the force of his arm to our cause. I swear, by the sword in my hand, that neither food nor drink shall pass my lips until I have discovered his fate.'

True to his word, Lugh departed from the battlefield that very evening, following the road which his father had taken. The moon was shining brightly in the sky by the time that he reached the northern plain, where Cian had met his end. There was no outward sign of the struggle, but a voice from below the earth brought Lugh and his companions to a halt.

'Unhappy Lugh,' came the voice, deep and solemn, 'your father lies beneath your feet. Here was he slain by the wretched sons of Tuireann. Bring me vengeance, my son. That is my last request of you.'

Swiftly, Lugh and his companions scrabbled in the dirt, hunting for Cian's body. Minutes later, they found it and raised it out of the ground. Lugh was appalled when he saw the condition of the corpse, all bloodied and scarred from a thousand wounds. Tenderly he bore it away and carried it home. There, it was buried with dignity and an ogham marker placed upon the grave-mound.

After these things were done, Lugh travelled to Tara with vengeance in his heart. His arrival coincided with a time of great feasting and rejoicing, for no report of Cian's murder had yet been made public and the Irish were celebrating the victory over the Fomorians. Lugh took his place of honour beside the king, but he sat solemn-faced throughout the entire banquet. His expression grew even more sombre when he saw that the children of Tuireann were in the hall.

At length, when the feasters had eaten their fill, Lugh rose to his feet and turned to address the company. 'My lords, I have a question to put to you all. What revenge would you take against the man who killed your father?'

A stunned silence fell on the assembly. 'What does this mean?' asked the king. 'Surely your father is not dead?'

'He is indeed,' replied Lugh, 'and the men who murdered him are here in this hall.'

The king was deeply shocked. 'If any man should slay my father, I would have him die a slow and agonizing death. Rather than kill him with a single stroke, I would cut off a single limb on successive days, until he begged me for mercy.' A murmur of agreement spread throughout the hall.

'Would it seem just to you then, if I were to claim nothing more than a blood-price for my father's life?' enquired Lugh.

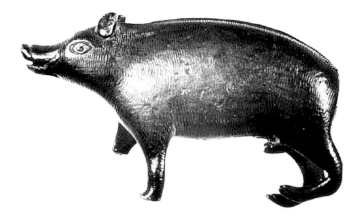

'That would be more than fair,' agreed the king. 'If I had committed such a terrible act, I would be extremely relieved if you were willing to accept an eric-fine from me.'

As they listened to these comments, the children of Tuireann spoke amongst themselves. Iuchair and Iucharba were convinced that Lugh must have discovered their guilt, and they were anxious to accept his generous terms. Brian was more suspicious. He thought that Lugh just wanted them to confess in front of the Tuatha Dé Danaan and that, once this had been done, he might refuse to accept a blood-price from them. Nevertheless, his brothers were insistent, so eventually he stood up and spoke, choosing his words carefully: 'It is clear that these accusations are levelled against us, since it is well known that a bitter enmity exists between our families. We will make no comment on the death of Cian but, as a matter of honour, we are willing to pay you an eric-fine for him.'

Lugh ignored the evasion. 'I shall accept your offer of a blood-price,' he said, 'though I am sure that you thought I would not. My fine is in seven parts: the first is three apples; the second is a spear; the third is two steeds and a chariot; the fourth is seven pigs; the fifth is a hound; the sixth is a cooking spit; and the seventh is three shouts on a hill. Is that fair? If it seems excessive, then speak now and I may reduce it. Otherwise, I demand that the fine be paid in full.'

'It does not seem too great at all,' answered Brian. 'Indeed, it appears so lenient that I expect some trickery in this matter. Even so, we accept your demands.'

'Very well then,' boomed Lugh triumphantly. 'You have agreed before all this company that you will pay my blood-price and I, for my part, confirm that I will seek no further vengeance for my father's death. Now I must give you further details of your fine. The three apples that I want are in the Garden of Hisberna, in the east of the world, and no other apples will do. Their skin is the colour of honey, and their taste can cure a warrior of all his wounds. In addition, the apples may be used as hurling weapons, for nothing can destroy them and they will always return to the thrower upon command. You will not find it easy to win these treasures, however, for it has long been prophesied that three young champions from the west would come to steal them. As a result, the king of Hisberna has set powerful guards to watch over them.

'The spear that I mentioned is the fabled spear of King Pezar of Persia. Fire and venom spring from its head, and it is known as the Slaughterer, because of the havoc that can be wreaked with it in times of war. When not in use, its fiery point is submerged in a great cauldron of water, to keep it from burning down the royal palace. The horses and the chariot belong to King Dobar of Siogair and nothing can match them for speed, either on land or on water. As to the pigs, they are the property of King Easal of the Golden Pillars. They can be killed and eaten on any evening, yet on the morrow they will be well again, ready for the next feast. What is more, anyone who tastes their flesh will be cured of all their maladies.

'The whelp is known as Fail-Inis, and it belongs to Ioruaidh, the king of the Cold Country. No other hound can run as fast, and the beasts of the forest fall dead at the sight of it. The cooking spit can be found on the island of Fincara, where it is guarded by thrice fifty warlike women. Woe to any warrior who crosses swords with them, for their weapons bear an enchantment. Any man who receives a wound will be forced to remain their forever.

'Finally, the three shouts must be uttered on the Hill of Midkena, to the north of Lochlann. Midkena and his sons watch over this hill, and they are under a *geis* to maintain absolute silence there. What is more, they are the warriors who instructed my father in the arts of war and, even if I were to forgive you for his death, they would not. At their hands, sons of Tuireann, you will surely meet your doom, even if you succeed in every other respect. Thus will I be avenged on you.'

After these words, Lugh took his place once more. The sons of Tuireann said nothing. They were too shocked and dumbfounded to make any response. Then did they truly regret the injuries that they had laid upon Cian.

THE THEFT OF THE MAGIC APPLES

After hearing the severity of Lugh's demands, the sons of Tuireann went straight to their father, to ask his advice on how they should obtain the eric-fine. Tuireann looked gloomy when he heard the news. 'Your plight is indeed dreadful,' he admitted, 'for no man alive can secure all those items and yet survive. Even so, you have a slender chance. Many of the articles are awesome weapons, which could be of great use to Lugh in his coming battles. He may be prepared to offer you assistance in obtaining these, while still remaining confident that you will meet your end on the Hill of Midkena. Why not go to him and ask to borrow Manannán's flying steed, Enbarr of the Flowing Mane, or at the very least, his magic currach. Either of these would help you travel the long distances that are necessary for your quest.'

The brothers could see the wisdom of these words and, without further ado, they went and put this request to Lugh. 'I cannot lend you Enbarr,' he said immediately, 'for it does not belong to me. However, I will give you permission to use my currach, the Wave-sweeper, for I am sure that it will only bring you to your end more quickly.'

Thus equipped, the brothers entered the magical currach and embarked on their quest. Swiftly, they paddled out to the open sea. There, Brian gave the vessel its instructions. 'Sweeper of the Waves, you are under our command. Take us without delay to the Garden of Hisberna.'

Only then did the marvel of Lugh's currach become apparent. It moved of its own accord, picking up speed rapidly, as it sailed at an astonishing rate through dangerous currents, narrow straits and treacherous sea-chasms. Within the space of an hour, it had brought the three brothers to the land of Hisberna.

'Now that we are here,' said Brian, 'how shall we obtain the apples, for we know that they are closely guarded?'

'Let us take them through force of arms,' said Iuchair, 'for are we not the fiercest and most skilful warriors in Ireland? Besides, the burden of our punishment is so heavy that it might be better for us to perish here, rather than prolong our hardships.'

'That is poor thinking, brother,' said Brian, 'for a warrior's skill requires as much cunning as bravery. I suggest that we turn ourselves into the shape of hawks and swoop down upon the trees. Doubtless, the guards will hurl their spears at us but, once we have evaded these, the apples will be ours for the taking.'

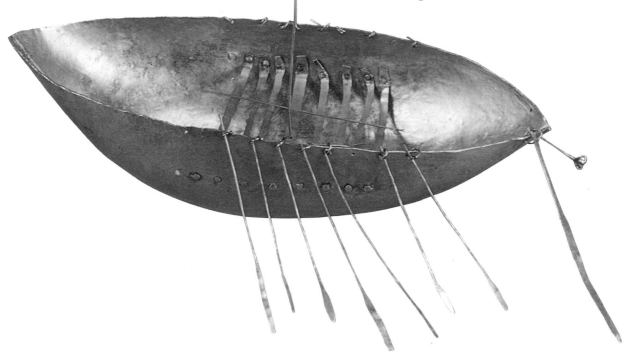

The others agreed that this was sound advice and Brian's plan was adopted. With his druid's rod, he changed the three of them into sleek, sharp-eyed hawks and they began to circle round the garden. As Brian had predicted, the guards soon spotted the intruders and hurled poisoned darts at them. But the birds were so alert that they evaded every single one. Then, as soon as the guards had run out of weapons, each of the brothers descended swiftly and plucked an apple with his beak. Immediately, they turned westwards, heading back to the sea as quickly as their wings could carry them.

News of the daring theft soon reached the palace of Hisberna. With loud cries, the king lamented the loss of his magic apples. His three daughters, however, were less willing to admit defeat. Swiftly, the wily maidens transformed themselves into griffins and gave chase. Then, as they drew close to the hawks, they provided an awesome demonstration of their powers. From their eyes, searing blue flames shot out towards the birds, scorching their wings. Iuchair and Iucharba were greatly afraid, convinced that the next bolt of fire from the griffins would consume them. Brian, however, remained calm. Through his druidic sorcery, he changed the brothers from hawks into fish, and they plummeted down into the sea below. The suddenness of this transformation confused the griffins and they gave up the chase. Much relieved at their narrow escape, the children of Tuireann returned to their human shapes and climbed into Lugh's boat. The first part of their quest had been completed successfully.

THE SEARCH FOR THE SLAUGHTERER

The apples of Hisberna came in useful when the brothers moved on to Persia, to undertake the next stage of their mission. Once again, they felt obliged to use some trickery, for it was well known that the king kept his spear in a closed room of the palace.

'How should we approach the king?' asked Brian of his brothers.

'Let us present ourselves in our true guises, as bold champions from Ireland,' said the others.

'No, I think that would be a mistake,' chided the elder brother. 'Let us rather go as learned poets, for they are held in much higher esteem. That way, we may gain ready access to the king's presence.'

Iuchair and Iucharba were sceptical, having no skill in verse, but they eventually accepted Brian's suggestion. So, all three tied their hair in the style of poets and approached the royal palace. There, they were ushered into the king's chamber.

'Greetings upon you, rhymesters of Ireland,' declared Pezar. 'Have you some verses for me?'

'We have,' said Brian, embarking on a lengthy poem, which compared King Pezar with his spear. 'Which is more powerful,' declaimed the poet, 'the honour of the king or the yew-wood of his spear; which is more deadly in battle, the strength of Pezar's right arm or the keen point of the Slaughterer; which shines more brightly, the glory of the king or the flaming brand of his magic spear?'

When Brian had finished his oration, the king was generous in his appraisal of its worth. 'That is a fine poem, man of Ireland, though I do not understand why you give such prominence to my spear.'

'Because that is the reward which I seek for my verses,' Brian replied.

The smile instantly vanished from Pezar's face. 'That is a very foolish request, for none may ask for the Slaughterer without forfeiting their lives. Indeed, the best reward that I could give you for your verse would be to allow you to leave this chamber unharmed.'

An air of tension gripped the palace. Pezar's guards reached for their swords, ready to strike upon the royal command. Brian, however, remained calm and made no attempt to defend himself. Instead, he reached inside his tunic and drew out one of the golden apples of Hisberna. The company gasped at the beauty of the object and the king leaned forward in his throne, thinking that the young man was about to offer him this token.

Instead, Brian drew back his arm and hurled the apple at the king. Like a speeding javelin, it shattered Pezar's brow and pierced his brain. Then, dislodging itself, the apple flew back, returning to Brian's hand.

The king's attendants were appalled at this act and rushed to tend their fallen king. Meanwhile, amid the confusion, the sons of Tuireann slipped out of the chamber and began to hunt for the spear. It did not take long. They found it in a separate room, with its head submerged in a huge, bronze vat of foaming liquid. The water bubbled fiercely and the room was thick with scalding steam.

Swiftly, Brian drew out the fabled spear from its resting place and raised it aloft. Then the brothers walked calmly through the palace and headed towards their boat. In spite of their attack on Pezar, they were perfectly safe. No one dared to challenge them, knowing full well that a single blow from the Slaughterer would bring them certain death.

THE TRICKERY OF LUGH

From Persia, the children of Tuireann moved on to the island of Siogair, to fulfil the next stage of their quest. This time, they posed as exiled warrior chieftains, seeking employment in a foreign king's command. By this means, they gained Dobar's confidence, until he proudly displayed his steeds and chariot before them. Then the brothers launched their attack, catching their opponent completely unawares. As in Persia, the royal guards attempted to protect their master. But, with the aid of Pezar's blazing spear and the apples of Hisberna, it was not long before the children of Tuireann won the day.

By this time, reports of the brothers' deeds and their fearsome armoury were spreading far and wide. Because of this, there was great consternation among the kings of many a distant land, each hoping that Lugh's blood-price would not bring the sons of Tuireann to his shores. This, in turn, lightened the burden on the brothers'

backs. For, when they came to tackle King Easal of the Golden Pillars about his seven pigs, they found him all compliance. The same thing happened in the Cold Country, when they sought the hound called Fail-Inis. King Ioruaidh handed it over without a murmur.

'This quest becomes ever easier,' rejoiced Iuchair, 'for, with each article that we gain, our force becomes stronger and our enemies less willing to do battle. At this rate, we must surely meet Lugh's demands without losing our lives.'

These words would return to haunt the son of Tuireann. For Lugh, too, had heard of the rapid progress of his enemies and was determined to halt it. With a cunning conjuration, he placed a spell upon the brothers, making them believe that they had collected all the items he had listed. This filled the three children of Tuireann with joy. Immediately, they gave orders to the Wave-sweeper to return them to Ireland, so that they could deliver their blood-price to Lugh and be free of their obligations to him.

Upon their arrival, the brothers went directly to the plain of Tara, where a royal fair was being held. Crowds gazed in wonder as they saw the remarkable booty, which Brian and his kinsmen had brought back for Lugh. The sons of Tuireann made their way through this throng and approached the king. He, too, congratulated the brothers on their success and sent his messengers to fetch Lugh. The latter, however, was nowhere to be found.

At this, Brian became scornful, 'I know perfectly well what has happened. Lugh has heard of our return and has gone into hiding, fearing that we will use this terrific arsenal against him.'

Moments later, though, Lugh's personal envoy arrived before the king. He conveyed his master's apologies for his delay, and asked the brothers to present the blood-price to the king. He himself would arrive shortly, to accept the eric-fine and discharge the brothers from their obligations.

This was done forthwith. Amid gasps of admiration, the children of Tuireann laid out their goods before the king. First, they brought Pezar's spear, the Slaughterer, holding it aloft for all the company to see, before dousing its flame in a cauldron of bubbling water. Next, they brought the steeds and chariot of King Dobar, racing them around the plain so that everyone could marvel at their speed. After this came the pigs, which had belonged to King Easal of the Golden Pillars, and the hound of King Ioruaidh. Finally, they brought out the apples from the Garden of Hisberna, which gleamed as brilliantly as the midday sun. All these things were laid out before the king, and the people of the Tuatha Dé Danaan clustered round to gaze upon these treasures.

Then Lugh arrived at the plain. With perfect grace, he watched as the king's servants brought the articles of his blood-price before him. He also accepted the return of the Wave-sweeper, which the children of Tuireann had borrowed from him. At length, he spoke: 'Here is indeed a marvellous array of gifts, enough to pay the blood-price of any mortal man. But, my lords, you know full well that an eric-fine must be paid in full, right down to the very last coin. So tell me, pray, where is the cooking-spit that I demanded? What of the three shouts on the Hill of Midkena? I asked you in the banqueting hall if you thought the price too great and you expressed yourselves content. Does your courage fail you now? If not, then give me my blood-price in full.'

Now the enchantment fell off the sons of Tuireann and they realized that they had been tricked. Lugh had all the parts of his eric-fine that could be of use to him. For how could a cooking-spit or three shouts be of service to him in times of war? What is more, they would now have to face the final part of their quest without their magic weapons. A sombre mood came upon the brothers at that moment, for they could see no way to escape from Lugh's unquenchable thirst for revenge.

THE FINAL PERILS OF THE QUEST

Once they had taken leave of their families, the three brothers set out to find the island of Fincara. The voyage was long and arduous, for they no longer had the benefit of Lugh's currach. Indeed, they were at sea for a full quarter of a year, braving terrible storms and perilous whirlpools, and in all that time they could find no one who knew of the island's location.

At last, in a remote corner of the Western Ocean, they came across a blind seer, all bent and wizened with age. He told the brothers that he had heard tidings of Fincara long ago, in the days of his youth. The joy of the brothers turned to despair, however, when the ancient informed them that the island lay not on the surface of the waters, but deep within its denizens. According to him, a cruel spell had caused Fincara to sink beneath the waves, along with all of its inhabitants.

Despite these ominous tidings, the brothers persisted in their quest. Following the old man's directions, they sailed out to where the island had last been sighted. Then, donning his water-apparel and his helmet of transparent crystal, Brian leapt over the side of the boat and began his search. This proved no easy task. For fourteen days, he wandered on the ocean's floor, looking for traces of the lost city. At last, signs of habitation came into view: a row of houses, all decked out with shells; a large enclosure, with trails of seaweed winding round the wooden staves; and, last of all, a fairy palace, encrusted with pearls and other treasures of the sea.

Brian went inside. Immediately, he found himself in a large and impressive hall, with an imposing oaken table at the centre. Upon this lay the cooking-spit that he was seeking. He was not alone, however, for a group of sea-maidens were seated round the table, stitching their needlework. Behind them, a row of female warriors stood ready, each carrying a sword or spear. All eyes were sternly fixed on Brian, as he walked slowly towards the table. Now, too late, he realized that he had devised no special plan for this moment. Instead, he lunged forward desperately and grabbed the cooking-spit, hoping that he would be able to outrun its owners. But there was no hostility. The women of Fincara simply burst out laughing. 'You are brave indeed, young warrior, for there are thrice fifty maidens here, and even the weakest among us could have prevented this act. Still, we applaud you for your bravery and will let you have the spit, for we have many others like it.'

Thankful for this generous gesture, Brian bade farewell and returned to his brothers with the prize. They did not rejoice overmuch, for they knew that the most dangerous of their tasks lay ahead.

Now it was time to travel to the north of Lochlann, to the Hill of Midkena. Midkena himself was awaiting their arrival and, when he saw the dust of their horses in the distance, he called on his sons to arm themselves. At last, the two families confronted each other. Midkena did battle with Brian, while his children – Aedh, Corc and Conn – attacked Iuchair and Iucharba. Long and hard was the fighting, with every man receiving blows from sword and spear. Finally, as the day was drawing to a close, Brian raised his sword for one supreme effort. Down came the blade, right through Midkena's helmet and skull, splitting his head in twain. Inspired by this sight, Iuchair and Iucharba launched themselves upon their foes with renewed frenzy. Soon, the sons of Midkena had joined their father in the long sleep of death.

Now, in their moment of victory, the children of Tuireann began to feel the severity of their wounds. Together, they collapsed upon the hill, bloody and exhausted, remaining there until a heavy curtain of darkness fell over their eyes.

Brian was the first to revive. In a feeble voice, he called out to his brothers, urging them to raise their spirits and climb a little way up the hill, to make the shouts that they had promised. This was a matter of honour, he knew, for each of them lay close to death. Still, determined that Lugh should not come gloating over their failure, the brothers crawled up the slope to utter their shouts, though these were little more than the hoarsest of whispers.

After this, Brian struggled to lead his brothers back to their ship and they left for home. Iuchair and Iucharba prayed that the sight of their native land might bring them new strength, while Brian had a more tangible hope for their salvation. He said nothing of this, however, until they reached their father's house. There, Tuireann lamented at his children's wounds, feeling sure that these would bring them to their death. Then Brian interrupted him. 'Beloved father, do us this one favour. Carry the cooking-spit of the Fincara women to Lugh, and tell him that we have uttered three shouts on the Hill of Midkena. With luck, the payment of his blood-price may ease his anger against us. If that is so, then crave a boon of him. Ask if he will lend us the apples of Hisberna. With these, we may heal our wounds and be well again.'

Immediately Tuireann went to Tara, where he sought out Lugh and gave him the cooking-spit. Then, just as his son had suggested, he asked the latter if he would lend him the golden apples. Lugh stared long and hard at the old warrior, taken aback by his request. But then he remembered the terrible wounds of Cian and he gave his decision in a stony voice: 'You may not have the apples, Tuireann. Indeed, I would not let you have them, even if you could turn the full compass of this land to gold and bestow it all on me. Your sons committed a wicked and pitiless deed and, for that, nothing short of their deaths will satisfy me.'

Tuireann returned home and gave his sons the dreadful news. Then Brian and his brothers knew that their fate was sealed and, shortly afterwards, they died. Tuireann buried them together, in a single grave. In death, as in the perils of their quest, they would not be parted from each other.

Fantastic Voyages

AS AN ISLAND RACE, the Irish were naturally curious about the wondrous lands which lay out in the far corners of the ocean. This gave rise to a specialized body of literature, the Immrama (literally 'rowing about'), which dealt with fabulous voyages into the unknown.

Some echoes of this can be found in the early myths. Tir na nÓg, the magical land of eternal youth, was one of a number of earthly paradises, visited by the Irish heroes. Others included Tir Tairrngire (the Land of Promise) and Mag Mell (the Plain of Pleasure). Most locations were characterized by endless feasting and revelry, and mortals could only gain access to them if they were conveyed there by one of the fairy people.

Equally popular with the storytellers was the notion of a land or city under the sea. In Ireland, this was usually called Tir fa Tonn (the Land beneath the Wave), although there were

Stone font from Clonfert Cathedral
Brendan's travels brought him to an island populated by strange spirits, trapped in the form of birds.

many variants. The island of Fincara, which is featured in the tale of *The Punishment of the Children of Tuireann*, was one of these, and there are obvious affinities with the legendary Breton city of Ys and Plato's lost continent of Atlantis. Often, the sunken lands were held under an enchantment and would rise again, if certain conditions were met.

THE ADVENTURES OF BRAN

The Immrama expanded greatly upon these magical visions. The oldest of these stories dates back to the eighth century and relates the adventures of Bran, son of Febal. In a dream, he is approached by a beautiful woman, who bids him come and find her. Spellbound by this vision, Bran sets out immediately with thrice nine companions. Their travels bring them to the domain of the sea-god Manannán and a number of mystic islands, before they finally arrive at the Land of Women. There, they spend a carefree existence for many years, before deciding to return to Ireland. Like Oisin, however, they find that they cannot land without suffering the pangs of old age. So, Bran writes his tale on ogham wands and casts them ashore, before turning back to sea.

The story of Bran is essentially pagan, although there are a few ecclesiastical interpolations. The spirit of the other Voyages, however, is decidedly Christian. The best of these is the Voyage of Maeldun, which probably dates from the ninth century and which many critics regard as the Irish Odyssey. The hero was the bastard son of Ailill Ochair Aga ('Edge of Battle') and a dishonoured nun. In due course, Ailill was slain by foreign marauders and Maeldun set out to avenge him. His lengthy wanderings took him

Gyrena

Miniature of St Brendan and a siren
The voyage of Brendan was a spiritual journey, in which the saint encountered many evil temptations.

filled with a compulsion to do the same and Maeldun was forced to abandon him. Other episodes had a Christian emphasis, as the voyagers came across hermits and pilgrims, who were kept alive by ministering angels. Then, when the travellers finally returned to Ireland, they placed their treasures on the altar of Armagh.

Maeldun's adventures appear to have been the main source for the Voyage of St Brendan, which gained immense popularity in the Middle Ages. Brendan (*c*.486–*c*.575) was a historical figure, who was raised in the west of Ireland by St Ita and founded the monastery of Clonfert. By the standards of the time, he travelled widely, visiting St Columba in Scotland and St Malo in Brittany. This reputation may have inspired the expatriate Irish monk, who wrote the story in the tenth century.

to more than thirty different islands, bringing him into contact with a host of dangerous beasts and magical snares.

On one island, for example, they found a hoard of treasure, guarded by a seemingly innocuous cat. As the Irishmen approached, however, the cat leapt through one of the men, reducing him to a heap of ashes. On another island, they noticed a group of people wailing and moaning helplessly. When one of the party went ashore to investigate, however, he was

The adventures of Brendan the Navigator took him to a variety of exotic locations. He visited an island inhabited by giant smiths and another, populated by bird-like spirits. Stranger still was the island of Jasconius, which turned out to be the back of an enormous whale. The tales of St Brendan were translated into many languages – among them German, Flemish, Italian and Norse – and they have survived in no fewer than one hundred and sixteen medieval manuscripts.

The Fate of the Children of Lir

AOIFE'S CURSE

After the Battle of Tailltin, where the Tuatha Dé Danaan were defeated by the Milesians, the survivors assembled to choose themselves a king. For, they reasoned, it was better to submit to the authority of one supreme leader than to remain a weak and divided people.

Now the chief contenders for this honour were Bodb and Oenghus, two of the Dagda's sons, Midir the Proud, Ilbrec of Assaroe, and Lir of Síd Finnachaid. After much deliberation, the choice fell upon Bodb, partly because of his virtue and partly because he was the Dagda's eldest son. Everyone applauded this decision, apart from Lir. In a fit of rage, he stormed out of the assembly, without pledging his allegiance to the new king. This petty act caused much offence, and many of the chieftains resolved to pursue Lir to his home and burn it to the ground. But Bodb forbade this,

for he knew that Lir would defend his land fiercely and hundreds of his new subjects would be slain.

For many a year this argument remained unmended, until a terrible tragedy occurred in Lir's household. His wife died suddenly and he was overcome with sorrow. When news of this reached Bodb's ears, he saw it as an opportunity for making peace between them. Messengers were sent to Síd Finnachaid, offering the hand of friendship. More than this, Bodb proposed that Lir should take one of his three foster-daughters – Aobh, Aoife and Arbha – to replace the wife that he had lost.

Lir was greatly moved by such generosity. Immediately, he set out from home with a company of fifty chariots, never stopping till he reached the royal palace. There, his arrival was greeted with much rejoicing and a feast was set before him. Then, on the morrow, he was introduced to the three maids and asked to make his choice.

'They are all beautiful,' said Lir, 'and I cannot say which is the worthiest. But I will take the eldest, for she must be blessed with nobility and wisdom.' In this way, his choice fell upon the fair Aobh and she became his bride. For fourteen days, the couple remained as the king's guests and lavish was the hospitality bestowed upon them. After this, they travelled home to Síd Finnachaid, where the celebrations continued until the end of the year.

The marriage proved a very happy one and, in due course, it was blessed with children. Aobh gave birth to twins, a boy and a girl, and they were given the names Aedh and Finola, which meant 'Fire' and 'White-shoulder'. Some time later, Aobh conceived again, bearing another pair of twins. These two sons were called Fiachra and Conn, and both were strong and healthy. But

the occasion of their birth was clouded with sorrow, for Aobh fell sick and died in labour. Once again, Lir was cast into a mood of black despondency and, without the comfort of his four little children, he might easily have been overcome by grief.

Lir's sense of loss was shared by Aobh's foster-father, Bodb and all his people. Throughout the king's household, there was deep sadness at Aobh's death, for she had been much loved during her childhood days at the royal palace. Then, when the period of mourning was over, Bodb addressed his people thus:

'We have grieved long and piteously for our dear foster-child, partly on account of her own sweet nature and partly out of love for the man to whom we gave her, for we appreciate his friendship and loyalty. This bond must not be broken. We have therefore decided to bestow upon him the hand of our second foster-child, Aoife. In place of the wife that was lost, let him now have her sister.'

Immediately, messengers were sent to Síd Finnachaid, to inform Lir of this bountiful act. He consented at once, thanking Bodb profusely for his kindness. Without delay, he departed for the king's house, there to be joined with his new bride. The wedding festivities were grand and dignified although, in the circumstances, they could hardly be as joyous as the celebrations he had enjoyed with Aobh.

Nevertheless, the early days of the marriage were promising. Aoife nursed her sister's children tenderly and appeared to love them as her own. Bodb, too, showed great affection for the infants. Many was the time he would travel to Síd Finnachaid to see them. On other occasions, he would send for the children to be brought to his palace, where he kept them for as long as he could, lamenting greatly when they had to leave his side. Nowhere was his love more plain than at the Feast of Age, the special ceremony which allowed the Tuatha Dé Danaan to remain free from sickness and decay. For here, at this auspicious event, the youngsters were given pride of place beside the king, and all the company agreed that these were the fairest children in Ireland.

Now when Aoife saw the attention lavished upon Lir's offspring, her love for them began to curdle. She felt that she was being neglected on their account. Gradually, as her jealousy and resentment turned to hatred, she started to dream of revenge. So powerful did these feelings become, that she feigned sickness and took to her bed. For a full twelve months, Aoife lay there brooding, planning her mischief. Only when her mind was made up did she rise from her bed and resume her role as the children's mother.

Aoife was well aware that, if she was to rid herself of these tiresome burdens, she would first have to separate them from their father. So, when the time came for their next visit to Bodb, she offered to take them. Lir consented willingly but, at the last moment, Finola refused to make the journey. For it had been revealed to her in a dream that she and her brothers were in peril. Lir calmed her fears, however, saying that these were nothing more than phantoms of the night, and eventually she agreed to go.

At the appointed time, Aoife had her chariot prepared and her attendants made ready, and the party set off towards Bodb's palace. They had reached Lake Darvra before she showed her true colours. Now Aoife took her minions aside and bade them kill the children. 'Put them to death,' she said, 'and you shall have all the worldly wealth that you desire. For I have lost the affection of my lord on their account, and can never regain it till they are gone.'

Aoife's servants were horrified when they heard this command, and refused to obey their mistress. So she took hold of a sword from one of them, thinking to do the job herself, but her woman's weakness held her back and she could not do the deed. Instead, she led the children to the shores of the lake and told them to bathe in its waters. This they were content to do, little suspecting the harm that it might bring them. For, as they walked into the lake, Aoife tapped the waters with a druid wand. Immediately, a wind swirled up around them and the youngsters gave out a terrible moan that rent the air, as they felt themselves being torn out of their bodies. Within moments, their childish forms had disappeared and Lir's unfortunate offspring had been transformed into four beautiful, snow-white swans.

Aoife gloated at her success. 'Away with you, you cursed creatures. Make what you can of your new home here on Lake Darvra, for you will never return to your old ways. Though your friends may rail at me or plead for mercy, nothing can be done. I have led you to your doom.'

The children of Lir listened to these words in dismay; for, although they were now swans, they could still speak and understand the words of humans. Finola swam across to her stepmother and cried out: 'Why have you done this to us, evil woman? We never sought to do you harm. Why has your friendship turned to treachery? Surely, if there is justice in this world, this crime will be avenged and you will suffer pains far worse than ours. But take pity! Change us back or, at the very least, let us know how long we must remain in this state.'

'That I can do,' said Aoife, 'though it will bring you little comfort. For three hundred years, you will linger here on the smooth waters of Lake Darvra; three hundred more must you spend amid the stormy waves of the Sea of Moyle, between Ireland and Scotland; and yet three hundred more upon the Western Sea at Inis Glora, where you will be buffeted by the icy breakers. Not until Lairgnen, the prince of the north, marries Deoch, the princess of the south, shall you know your freedom. Nor will it transpire before a holy man named Patrick, whom the druids know as Taillkenn, brings his teachings to this land. Only when you hear the sound of a Christian bell will you know that your release is close at hand. Until then, no power can set you free; not mine, nor Lir's, nor that of anyone who loves you.'

'Still,' she continued, in a milder tone, 'since it can avail you nothing, you may keep your human

voices. What is more, these voices will have the sweetness of the Sidhe in them and, when you sing, there will be no music in the world to match it. Any man who hears your song shall instantly be lulled into a soft and charmed slumber. That is the extent of my mercy. Now go! I never wish to see your faces more.'

With these words, Aoife turned away from the lake and returned to her chariot. Moments later, she was gone, thundering away towards the royal palace. The curse that she had laid was now in force, even down to her final wish. For, in the short time that was left to her, she never again saw the children of Lir.

THE SUFFERING OF THE SWANS

After the terrible atrocity which she had ruthlessly committed at Lake Darvra, Aoife hurried away, driving her chariot as quickly as she could. At the king's palace she was greeted warmly by all the household, as was customary. The rejoicing of Bodb and his people ebbed away, however, when they saw that Lir's offspring were not with her. More than this, their delight was replaced by anger, when they heard the reason for the children's absence.

'Lir no longer loves or trusts you,' she informed the king, 'and thus does not wish to leave his children in your care, fearing that you may hold them hostage.'

'How can this be so?' asked Bodb. 'Surely, it is plain to all that I love these children better than my own. No power on this earth could prevail upon me to do them harm.' Aoife merely shrugged when he spoke these words, so Bodb said nothing more. Secretly, though, he was suspicious, wondering if there might not be some treachery in this matter. So, while his foster-daughter rested, he sent his messengers hurrying northwards to Síd Finnachaid, to hear what Lir might have to say.

The arrival of these envoys troubled Lir greatly. He had assumed, of course, that the children were with Bodb and it caused him much anxiety to think that some mischief might have befallen them. Immediately, he made ready to journey with his

attendants to the royal stronghold. Soon, his chariot was speeding on its way.

It did not take long for him to draw near to Lake Darvra, where Aoife had worked her sorcery. From afar, the swans witnessed the dust of his cavalcade. 'How well I know the people of this band,' said Finola to her brothers. 'What sorrow we will bring to them, when they see us in our present state. Come, let us move closer to the shore, so that they may know what has happened.'

From the water's edge they called out a greeting to their father, who was now within earshot. At first, Lir was amazed to hear birds talking, thinking that some witchcraft was being performed on him. With wonderment, he asked the leader of the swans who they were and by what manner they had assumed their present form.

'Know, father, that we are your children,' said Finola. 'Our evil stepmother has given us these shapes out of malice and jealousy.'

When he heard these words, Lir fell to his knees and wept, and all his people cried out with him. 'Is there no way,' he asked, 'that this wickedness can be undone?'

'None at all,' replied Finola regretfully, and she went on to cite the prophecy that Aoife had given.

'If this must be,' said Lir, 'then come and rest upon my chariot. We shall return to Síd Finnachaid and there, at least, you may be consoled by the company of your friends and family.'

'That is not possible,' responded Finola. 'We may not leave these shores, not until three hundred years have passed.' Then Lir was truly sorrowful, for he saw that his children were lost to him. 'Take comfort,' his daughter continued. 'Stay with us tonight and we will chant our music for you.'

Lir nodded sadly and, turning to his people, he ordered them to make camp. After this was done, the swans began their sweet, fairy song, which was so soft and soothing that all who heard it were lulled into a gentle sleep.

Next day, Lir bade his children farewell and travelled on to see the king. At first, his reception was cool, since Bodb had hoped to see the children

with him. But, as Lir related his tragic tale, the king's mood turned to rage. Instantly, he gave orders that Aoife should be brought from her chamber. With sharp words, he reproached her for the evil that she had done, and promised that her punishment should exceed all her worst imaginings. Then, raising his druid's rod, Bodb struck her on the shoulder. Aoife let out a piercing shriek, as the enchantment took effect. In a moment she was altered, her body changed into a demon of the air, forced to drift helplessly among the clouds until the end of time.

Then Bodb and all the Tuatha Dé Danaan went back with Lir to Lake Darvra, to witness what Aoife had performed. As evening fell, they listened to the singing of the swans, wafting like a lullaby across the placid waters.

Throughout the ensuing years, this vigil at the lake became a common experience. Men came from every part of Ireland, to converse with the swans during the day and hear their balming melodies at night. And all who listened to their song forgot their pains, their sickness and their suffering, returning to their homes feeling refreshed and content.

So pleasant were these times that the years flew by painlessly for the swans. Then, one day, Finola turned to her comrades and said: 'Do you realize, my dear brothers, that we have come to the end of our season in this place? This night will be our last on Lake Darvra.' The news saddened her three companions, for they had felt almost as much at home on Darvra's waters as if they had been living in their father's house. Besides, they knew that on Moyle's wild sea they would be deprived of all human society, forced to lead a lonely existence with only each other for company.

Next morning, the four swans bade a lingering farewell to all their loved ones, unsure if they would ever see their faces again. Then the swans spread their wings and rose high into the air, flying northwards to the Sea of Moyle. The Tuatha Dé Danaan grieved heartily to see them go and, from that very day, they made it a crime for any man in Ireland to kill a swan.

Life on the Sea of Moyle – that icy stretch of water which separates Ireland from Scotland – proved every bit as gloomy as Finola had feared. The waters around them were dark and threatening, and their only view of Irish soil consisted of steep cliffs and jagged rocks. Hunger and cold were new perils, which had never troubled them in their inland home, but most of all they missed the sound of human talk and laughter. Now, truly, they felt the brunt of Aoife's cruelty, and their song turned to a plaintive lament, echoing away across the desolate sea.

The swans lived despairingly in this manner for many months until, one night, Finola noticed a fearful tempest brewing in the east. 'Dear brothers,' she said, 'this storm is coming fast upon us and will surely separate us. So, let us now appoint a meeting place, or it may happen that we shall never see each other again.'

The brothers agreed, and Fiachra suggested that they should make for Carricknarone, the Rock of Seals, since each of them was familiar with this spot. Midnight came and, with it, the full force of the tempest. Lightning flashed, thunder roared and squalls of wind threw the swans against the rocks, ripping many a feather from their wings. Soon, the children of Lir were scattered in all directions, little knowing which way was north and which was south.

At last, dawn broke and the storm abated. When the skies cleared Finola found that she was lost, many leagues away from her normal haunts. She also felt exhausted, following the battering she had taken during the night. Even so, she flew directly to the rendezvous. When she reached the Rock of Seals, she found to her horror that it was deserted. For one terrible moment, she feared that the others had perished, and that she would have to spend the rest of her captivity in solitude. 'How terrible life will be,' she thought, 'if I alone have survived. My feathers are numb with the cold, my pinions are almost torn away, but these things will be as nothing if I cannot see once more the brothers who have sheltered so often beneath my wings.' Finola waited all day on the Rock of Seals until, one by one, the others arrived, each looking more weary and bedraggled than his predecessor.

Many further hardships did the swans suffer over the coming years. One winter night, a dreadful frost descended on the Sea of Moyle, freezing the waters into a solid floor of ice. The children of Lir sheltered on Carricknarone that night, but this did not protect them from the elements. Instead, their feet and wings became frozen to the rock, almost rooting them to the spot. So powerful was this icy grip that the swans were forced to leave behind the skin from their feet and the tips of their quills, in order to escape. These injuries hurt them sorely, for every touch of salt water on their raw flesh made them cry out in agony, until they felt sure that they would die of pain.

In better times, the swans would explore along the deserted coastline, hoping for some fleeting glimpse of human company. Once, when they flew as far as the mouth of the Bann, they sighted a troop of horsemen riding along the shore. Snow-white were their steeds and brightly glittering their armour, as it glinted in the sun. Venturing nearer, they were delighted to find that these were men of the Tuatha Dé Danaan. Among them were the two sons of Bodb, Aedh the Quick-Witted and Fergus the Chess Player, together with many fine warriors from the Sidhe. They had been searching for the children of Lir for many a month, anxious to hear how they were faring.

For all too brief an hour, the birds remained with them, asking eagerly for news of their loved ones. 'The king and your father are both well,' replied the leader of the company. 'At this very moment, they will be at Síd Finnachaid, celebrating the Feast of Age. Be assured, their happiness will be complete, when we can report that we have seen you safe and well.'

Soon, the swans were forced to leave, for they were not permitted to stray too far from the icy Sea of Moyle. The horsemen, too, departed, happy to have completed their mission. At once, they brought the tidings to Lir's household, where it was received with a mixture of emotions: sorrow at the hardships which the birds were suffering, but relief that they were still alive and might one day be freed from their exile.

As for the children of Lir, they remained on the Sea of Moyle until they had fulfilled their allotted span of years. Then, at last, they were able to take wing and fly on to their final destination. This was the Western Sea, a spot no less remote and forbidding than their previous home.

While they were languishing in this dreadful place, they chanced upon a young man named Ebric, whose family owned a strip of land beside the shore. He heard their plaintive singing from afar and came down to the water's edge, to see what sort of creatures could make such a heavenly noise. For many a day, he stayed there and conversed with them, listening to their tale of woe. Then fierce winds rose up, tearing the birds away from the shore, and he saw them no more. After this, the young man hurried back to his people, telling them wondrous stories about the speaking swans of Ireland, and it is through Ebric's account that we know about the children of Lir today.

For their part, the swans soon discovered that life on the Western Sea was every bit as bleak as it had been in their previous home. Most terrible of all was one particular winter's night, when the entire surface of the sea, from Irros Domnann to Achill, hardened into a thick floor of ice. A bitter north-west wind hurled the birds about, until their screams and lamentations filled the air. Bravely, Finola tried to comfort her companions. 'Dearest brothers, you must believe in the God of truth, who

made all the fertile places of the earth and the wonders of the skies. Put your trust in Him, and He will bring you solace and comfort, to help you bear these hardships.'

'We believe in Him,' they echoed. And, from this time on, the children of Lir found a new strength, to guide them through their final trials. Henceforth, the storms and tempests seemed less violent, the winds less icy in their blasts. Thus fortified, they lingered by the Western Sea until the end of their ordeal lay in sight. For thrice three hundred years, they had been the helpless victims of Aoife's cruelty. Now, they hoped, their lives could begin again.

THE SPELL IS BROKEN

When their time upon the Western Sea was over, the first thought of Finola and her brothers was to return to their old home at Síd Finnachaid. With gladness in their hearts, they spread their wings and began to fly inland. The flight was long, but their spirits rose as they passed over places that they recognized from their youth. Before they knew it, the lofty mound of Lir came into view.

As they drew nearer, nostalgic thoughts were banished from their minds. For Síd Finnachaid had undergone a terrible transformation. Their father's palace was desolate and empty. The halls were ruined, all overgrown with brambles, weeds and banks of nettles. Not a house, nor a hearth, nor any other sign of human habitation had survived.

Finola voiced the horror which they shared: 'Oh brothers, what has happened here? Where is our father, whom we have ached to see? Where are the valiant heroes, who used to feast within this place? Where are the happy youths, who used to laugh and play with us? Where are the bright shields glittering on the walls, the sporting hounds ready for the chase, the silver goblets brimming with their potent brew? Is everyone we knew now stilled and dead? Is nothing left but this wild grass and rank decay?'

They remained that night amid the ruins of the palace, fondly remembering their lost childhood.

Irish Gods

THE VARIOUS DEITIES OF Irish mythology are less imposing, in many ways, than their counterparts in other European cultures. They are rarely worshipped or invoked by the heroes of the legends and, for all their undoubted powers, they are frequently shown to be fallible. Indeed, in some instances, it is hard to distinguish a god from a mortal.

The Irish pantheon appears to have been quite large, although much of the action in this volume is centred around a few, key figures. The most important of these is Lugh. His traditional

epithet – Lugh of the Shining Countenance – confirms that he was a solar deity. Evidence of this can be found in *The Birth of Cú Chulainn*, and also in the god's connection with the summer festival of Lughnasadh. According to legend, the latter coincided with a series of funeral games, which Lugh founded to honour the memory of his mother, Tailtu. These games were held at regular intervals, along the lines of the early Greek Olympics.

Lugh also manifested a number of other qualities. In *The Punishment of the Children of Tuireann*, he appears as a great warrior, winning the title of Lugh of the Long Arm. Here, his exploits help to free Ireland from the oppression

Plate from the Gundestrup Cauldron
One of a series of Celtic deities, portrayed on the outer plates of a ritual cauldron, discovered in a Danish peat bog.

of the Fomorians and establish the supremacy of the Tuatha Dé Danaan. He was also portrayed as a craft god, and the Romans seem to have equated him with the Gaulish Mercury. Eventually, this became his dominant aspect and there is a theory that he gave his name to the leprechaun, the fairy cobbler with the hoard of gold. Lugh was revered throughout much of Celtic Europe and his name can be linked with a number of cities, among them Lyon (Lugdunum), Leiden and Carlisle (Luguvalum).

THE DAGDA

After Lugh, the most prominent gods in the early myths were probably the Dagda and his sons, Bodb and Oenghus. The Dagda was revered as the father of the gods, playing a vital role as chief of the Tuatha Dé Danaan and patron of the druids. Above all, he was a fertility god, as his life-giving club and inexhaustible cauldron would suggest. He was the mate of Boann, a water spirit personifying the River Boyne.

Bronze figure of a god
At first glance, this resembles a Classical bust, but the tiny hoofed legs confirm that it is a Celtic animal god.

Bodb was the eldest son of the Dagda and succeeded him as leader of the Tuatha Dé Danaan, but he was largely overshadowed by Oenghus, the god of love. The latter was always described as young and handsome, with four birds hovering above his head. These represented his kisses and, when they began to sing, anyone within earshot fell hopelessly in love. Several stories deal with the assistance which Oenghus brought to amorous couples. In

The Wooing of Etain, he aided his foster-father while, in another tale, he helped Diarmaid, one of the leading warriors in the Fianna, when he eloped with Finn's future bride.

Two sea-gods, Lir and Manannán, also feature in the legends. The former is principally remembered for his role as the unhappy father in *The Fate of the Children of Lir* although, in this instance, he is a land-dweller. More famously, this god was probably also a distant source for Shakespeare's King Lear. Lir's son, Manannán, is a more complex character. On some occasions, he is visualized as a traditional marine god, riding the waves on a sea chariot with his wife, Fand, the Pearl of Beauty. At other times, he is portrayed as a shape-changer and magician, armed with an array of fabulous weapons. These included an invincible sword called the Answerer, which he bestowed on Lugh; a magical boat, the Sweeper of the Waves, which obeyed the thoughts of those who sailed in it; and a magnificent cloak, which could change into any colour. The Isle of Man is said to have been named after Manannán, because he used it as his throne.

The most sinister of the Irish deities was the Morrígán, a goddess of war and death, who hovered over battlefields and scavenged on dead warriors. She was a shape-shifter, usually appearing in her favourite guise as a crow or raven. She may be the prototype for the Morgan Le Fay of Arthurian legend. In the Ulster cycle, she became an implacable enemy of Cú Chulainn, helping to bring about his death.

At dusk, they sang their plaintive chants and all the birds of the neighbourhood flocked to hear them. Next morning, the swans flew off, for it gave them no pleasure to linger at the ruins of Síd Finnachaid. Instead, they returned to the island of Inis Glora on the Western Sea, knowing of no other place where they could make their home. Over the ensuing months, they explored the most distant points of this coastline. Once, they went to Iniskea, the Island of the Lonely Crane, where it is said that a solitary crane has dwelt since the beginning of time and will live on until the final day of doom.

On another occasion, they flew south to Tech Duinn, that bleak spot on a barren crag where the god of the dead is thought to reside. They no longer thought of their own condition, for what would it avail them now to become human once again?

The swans lived in this manner for many years, until St Patrick came to Ireland's shores and began to spread the word of God across the land. Other holy men followed in his wake, among them St Kennock, who founded an oratory on Inis Glora. One morning, the children of Lir heard the ringing of his matins bell and they started to tremble, for the sound was new and strange to them. The three brothers ran about wildly, flapping their wings, but Finola was more composed. 'Do you not understand the meaning of this noise?' she asked them.

'It is a low and fearsome voice,' they replied, 'but we do not know from whence it comes.'

'This is the voice of the Christian bell,' she explained, 'and it signals that our term of suffering is drawing to an end. God has willed it so.'

This allayed the brothers' anxieties and they listened to the music of the bell, until the hermit had finished matins. Then they began their own song, gentle and melodious, which drifted away on the morning breeze. Kennock was at prayer when he heard this chanting and, as he marvelled at the sweet sound, the Lord revealed to him that it came from the children of Lir. This delighted him, for he had already heard much of their tragic tale.

The following morning, Kennock went down to the water's edge and watched the four swans swimming together. As they came closer, he called out to them, asking if they were indeed the fabled offspring of Lir.

'Certainly, we are,' they replied in unison.

'I give thanks to God for that,' said Kennock, 'for it was on your account that I came to worship in this remote spot, in preference to all the other isles in Ireland. Come and walk with me now upon the land, for I swear to you that you will soon be freed from your enchantment.'

The swans were filled with joy on hearing these words, and they followed the holy man to his house. There, he summoned a skilled craftsman, bidding him fashion two silver chains of infinite delicacy. These he placed around the necks of the twins, joining Finola with Aedh and Fiachra with Conn. After this, the swans lived in Kennock's house, hearing him preach and joining in his devotions. This brought them such contentment that they quite forgot the long years of misery, which they had spent on Irish waters.

Now the ruler of Connacht at this time was King Lairgnen, the son of Colman, and his queen was Deoch, the daughter of the king of Munster. They had recently been married, thus fulfilling Aoife's prediction about the union of the north and the south. Deoch had heard much talk of the singing swans, with their mellifluent voices, and she was filled with a strong desire to possess them. So she went to the king and urged him to obtain the creatures for her, as part of her bridal present.

Lairgnen was unwilling to ask such a thing of Kennock, however, and he refused her request. This sent Deoch into a fury. Immediately, she stormed out of the palace, declaring that she would not spend another night in the place until Lairgnen had procured the swans.

When he learned of the queen's actions, Lairgnen relented. Messengers were despatched to her father's house, begging her to come home. Meanwhile, the king also sent word to Kennock on Inis Glora, asking him to deliver up the swans to the palace. But the envoys returned empty-handed. The swans, Kennock explained, were not insensate beasts, which could be sold or bartered. They were flesh and blood; human victims trapped in animal form by a wicked enchantment.

Lairgnen was outraged when he received this lecture. Without further ado, he journeyed to Inis Glora, to confront the holy man in person. Bursting into Kennock's chapel, he demanded to know why his command had been disobeyed. Then, without waiting for an answer, he began to drag the four swans away from the altar, pulling them by their silver chains.

The violence of Lairgnen's act had drastic consequences. As he tugged at the poor creatures, their bird-skins fell away and they were returned to human form. Where, a moment before, there had been four beautiful, snow-white swans, now there were three wizened old men and an ancient, silver-haired lady. Lairgnen was terrified, when he witnessed this transformation. Dropping the chains, he fled towards the door with Kennock's reproaches ringing in his ears.

Burdened with age, the offspring of Lir sank to the floor. With an effort, Finola called across to Kennock: 'Come, holy man, baptize us quickly, for we have not long to live. Do not grieve over us, for it is a relief to have shed our bird-like form at last. Only one thing more do I ask: bury us here together on Inis Glora, for we have spent some of our happiest days in your company.'

Kennock was obedient to her last wishes. The four were swiftly baptized and, shortly afterwards, they passed away. The holy man made their grave outside his chapel and, as Finola had requested, he buried them all together. She was at the centre, with Fiachra on her left, Conn on her right and Aedh resting before her face. Finola had chosen this arrangement, because it reminded her of those fearful times on the open, tumultuous seas, when she had sheltered her brothers beneath her wings.

After their burial, Kennock placed a pillar-stone on their grave-mound, bearing their names in ogham letters. Then, looking up, he beheld a radiant vision of four innocent children, each with silvery wings and joyous expressions on their faces. They smiled down at him for an instant, before spreading their wings and flying upwards towards heaven.

The Ulster Cycle

IRELAND'S MOST FAMOUS CYCLE of stories introduces a breed of fearless warriors. Chief among them is Cú Chulainn, the legendary Hound of Culann, who willingly exchanges a long life for a brief and glorious one. Magic surrounds his birth, which stems from the trickery of a god, but his many deeds encompass all that is most worthy and valiant in Ireland's mortal heroes. Cú Chulainn's adventures on Scáthach's Isle of Shadows, and the tasks which he performs to win his bride, bring him great renown throughout all of Ireland. No other feats, however, can match his wondrous exploits during the Cattle Raid of Cooley, when he alone holds the forces of Connacht at bay.

The Birth of Cú Chulainn

Now it happened on a certain day that Conchobar, the King of Ulster, was at his capital, Emain Macha, preparing for the marriage of his sister Dechtire. She was to wed a prince named Sualtam, who was the brother of Fergus Mac Roth. At the feast, Dechtire grew thirsty and took some wine. But, as she was drinking it, a mayfly flew into the cup and she swallowed it along with the wine. Soon after, she went into the parlour with her fifty maidens and fell into a sleep. And in this sleep, Lugh the god of light appeared before her, saying:

'I was that mayfly that came into your wine cup. Now you and your maidens must follow me.' Whereupon, he transformed them into of a flock of birds and they went south with him, to the fairy-dwelling at Brug na Bóinne. Here they remained, and no one at Emain Macha knew where they were or what had become of them.

About a year later, Conchobar and his nobles were gathered again at Emain, attending another feast. Suddenly, they spied through the window a great flock of birds, which descended onto the plain and began to feed upon the crops. They ravaged the land, leaving behind them not so much as a single blade of grass.

The men of Ulster were sorely vexed when they saw the birds destroying everything in their path. Swiftly, they yoked up their chariots and began to pursue them. Conchobar led the way and Fergus Mac Roth and poison-tongued Bricriu were among the company. The chase took them south and, as their chariots thundered through open country, they had to admire the beauty of the birds. There were nine flocks of them in all, linked in pairs by chains of silver. At the head of each flock, there were two birds of different colours, linked together by a chain of gold. In front of all of these, there were three birds which flew alone, leading the entire formation towards Brug na Bóinne.

Darkness fell and the birds vanished from the sky. Conchobar ordered his men to dismount and sent Bricriu to seek out shelter. All he could find, however, was a mean-looking house, where an old couple made him welcome. They bade him bring his companions to share their hospitality, but Bricriu was unimpressed. When he returned to Conchobar, he said that there would be little point in accepting the offer, unless they took their own provisions along.

Despite this, the men of Ulster went with Conchobar to the house. To their surprise, they found that it was large and well-appointed, very different from Bricriu's description. At the door, they were greeted by a young man with a shining countenance, dressed in a suit of armour. He ushered them in and led them to the feasting table. Food and drink of every kind awaited them there, and the lords of Ulster wasted no time in satisfying their appetites. When they had consumed every morsel, Conchobar turned to the young man and enquired after his lady: 'Where is the mistress of the house that she does not come to bid us welcome?'

'You cannot see her tonight,' was the reply, 'for she is in the pangs of child-birth.' And sure enough, later that night, the bawl of a newborn infant could be heard throughout the house. At the very same moment, a mare gave birth to two foals. And the men of Ulster took charge of the foals, meaning to present them as a gift for the child.

In the morning, Conchobar was the first to rise. He went to look for his host, but the man was nowhere to be seen. So, hearing the cry of a baby, he went to the mother's room. There he found Dechtire, with her maidens all around her and a child lying in her lap. And she welcomed Conchobar and explained to him all that had occurred; how she and her maidens had been spirited away from Emain Macha by Lugh, and how he had appeared before the Ulstermen as a young man dressed in armour.

Conchobar listened to all that Dechtire said, delighted to find his sister safe and well after so long an absence. And he praised her, saying: 'You have done well, Dechtire. You have given shelter to me and my chariots; you have kept the cold from my horses; you have given food to me and my people; and now you bring us this, the finest gift of all.'

The news was swiftly passed to the men of Ulster. They, too, were pleased, each one offering to raise the child and instruct him in their own special skills. Indeed, their arguments grew so fierce that Conchobar decided they should return to Emain, to consult Morann the Judge on the matter. His words were always respected, because the torc around his neck would tighten if he gave a false judgment. So it was agreed, and all the company travelled with Conchobar to his capital.

When they arrived there, Morann made his judgment. 'It is for Conchobar to raise the child, for he is next of kin to him. But let Sencha the Poet instruct him in speech and oratory; let Fergus the Warrior hold him on his knees; and let Amergin the Sage be his tutor.' And he added: 'This child will be praised by all, by chariot drivers and soldiers, by kings and seers. He will avenge all your wrongs; he will defend your fords; he will fight all your battles.'

And so it was settled. The child was taken to the plain of Muirthemne, where he spent his infant years with Dechtire and her husband Sualtam, before passing into the care of Conchobar. And the name he was given was Cú Chulainn, which means the Hound of Culann.

Cú Chulainn and Emer

THE WOOING OF EMER

As Cú Chulainn grew towards manhood, his skills in the arts of war became a source of wonder at Emain Macha. All the women of Ulster loved him for his strength, his handsome features and his fine way of speaking. They also admired his wisdom, his prudence in battle and his gifts of prophecy and judgment. Indeed, they could only find three faults in him – that he was too young, too brave and too beautiful.

The men of Ulster became concerned at Cú Chulainn's popularity and resolved to find a wife for him. Once he was married, they reasoned, there would be less danger of him turning the heads of their wives and daughters. Besides, it had been prophesied that he was to die young, and they thought it a shame that so great a warrior should leave no heir behind him. So, Conchobar sent nine men into each of the provinces of Ireland, to seek out a suitable mate for their hero. They looked in every town and every fort but, at the end of the year, they returned to Emain empty-handed.

Then Cú Chulainn himself went to Luglochta Loga, the Garden of Lugh. There, he met with a girl that he already knew. Her name was Emer, the daughter of Forgall Manach the Cunning. Of all the girls in Ireland, she was the most to his liking; for she had the six gifts – the gift of beauty, the gift of voice, the gift of sweet words, the gift of wisdom, the gift of needlework and the gift of chastity.

When Cú Chulainn arrived, Emer was sitting in the field with her maidens, schooling them in their needlework. She recognized him instantly, greeting him with these words: 'May the gods make all roads smooth before you.'

'And you,' he replied, 'may you keep safe from every harm.'

After this, they began to speak in riddles, so that the maidens would not understand them. And in their double-talk, Cú Chulainn made it plain to Emer that he wished to make her his wife.

His eyes observed the rise of her breasts, above the top of her dress. 'That is a fair country,' he said. 'How I might wish to wander there.'

Emer smiled, 'No man may travel there, unless he kills a hundred men at every ford between Ailbine and Banchuig Arcait.'

Cú Chulainn looked at her again and said, 'That is a fair country.'

'No man may travel there, until he has slain thrice nine men with a single stroke, sparing a single man in each group of nine.'

Once more, Cú Chulainn looked at her and repeated, 'That is a fair country.'

'No man may travel there, who has not gone sleepless from Samhain to the lambing time at Imbolc, and from Imbolc to the fiery season of Beltane, then again from Beltane to Lughnasadh, when the earth yields up its fruit, and finally round to Samhain time again.'

'Everything shall be as you command,' agreed Cú Chulainn.

'Then I accept the offer you have made me,' said Emer. And, with these riddling words, Cú Chulainn took his leave of the fair maiden and returned to Emain Macha.

After his departure, Emer's maidens went back to their homes and told their parents about the strange conversation they had witnessed at the Garden of Lugh. Their words, in turn, were reported to Forgall Manach and, although he could not understand the hidden meanings of their speech, he was suspicious of Cú Chulainn's motives. So, determined to hinder the boy's plans, he donned the disguise of a Gaulish chieftain and travelled to Emain Macha. There, he was warmly received by Conchobar and the men of Ulster.

For three days, there was feasting and drinking and, during this time, Forgall praised the fighting skills of his hosts. Above all, he praised Cú Chulainn for his feats and daring, adding that the young man would be well advised to journey to the island of Scáthach the Shadowy One. For surely, once he had completed his training under this great female warrior, no one in the world would dare to cross swords with him. Cú Chulainn leapt at the idea, promising to set out the very next day. Forgall smiled at this, for it was his hope that the young man would perish on the dangerous route to Alba and the Isle of Shadows, and would never return to marry his daughter.

CÚ CHULAINN ON THE ISLE OF SHADOWS

Before leaving for Scáthach's isle, Cú Chulainn travelled across to the plain of Breg, to make his farewells to Emer. She urged the young warrior to take care, explaining that it was Forgall's belief that he would never return alive from this perilous mission. Then they swore to be true to each other and, with this vow in his heart, Cú Chulainn turned his thoughts towards Alba.

Next day, he set sail from Ireland, taking with him King Conchobar, Laoghaire and Conall the Victorious as his companions. Their first stop was at the forge of Donall the Smith. There, they were taught how to blow his vast leather bellows and how to walk upon the fire, until their feet were cracked and blistered. During this interlude, the champions were observed by Donall's daughter, Dornolla of the Big Fist. Her appearance was fearsome to behold, for her face had been blackened by the soot of the forge and her hair was as red as its glowing embers. Now Dornolla's gaze fell upon Cú Chulainn and she loved him. The Ulsterman refused her, however, for his promise to Emer was still fresh in his mind. This enraged Dornolla and she swore to be revenged on him.

Shortly afterwards, the party decided to bid farewell to Donall and continue on their journey. At this point, Dornolla conjured up a vision of Emain Macha, borne high upon a golden cloud. Such was the beauty of this illusion that Cú Chulainn's companions could go no further. Dornolla's enchantment held them back and forced them to return home. In this way, Cú Chulainn was obliged to face the dangers of Scáthach's isle alone, just as Donall's daughter had intended.

Some time later, the Ulsterman landed on a bleak part of Alba's shores. Now he felt truly lost, and longed for the fellowship of his comrades. This mood did not linger long, however, for he soon became aware that a powerful beast was blocking his way. This creature had the wild look and fierceness of a lion, but its tail was made of thorny spikes and its breath came out like fire. The beast did not attack Cú Chulainn, but neither would it let him pass. Whenever he moved, it bounded in front of him and bared its teeth. At length, the warrior took a mighty leap and jumped upon its back. Instantly, the creature turned and ran inland, and Cú Chulainn had no means of controlling it. For four days, the beast carried him on its back, until it reached the edge of a lake, where it came to a halt. Cú Chulainn climbed down and, as he did so, the animal scurried away. Soon, it was gone and Cú Chulainn saw it no more.

From here, a winding path led through the Plain of Ill Fortune, where the blades of grass clung to men's feet, holding them fast until they perished. Cú Chulainn picked his way carefully through this inhospitable terrain, until he came upon a band of warriors. Now he knew that he was close to his journey's end, for these were the students of Scáthach. Among their company were faces that he recognized from his native land. Naoise was there, together with the other sons of Usnach, and so was Ferdia, the valiant son of Daire. Cú Chulainn greeted them with a wave, and asked them where he might find Scáthach. They smiled knowingly and pointed to a nearby island.

'You must cross over to it by the Novices' Bridge,' they cried, 'for only when you have passed that test will she consider you worthy of her teachings.'

The bridge in question was a curious construction for, whenever anyone stepped on it, the far side would rear up and throw him on his back. Three times Cú Chulainn tried to cross it but on each occasion, he was hurled to the ground. The others jeered at him and this incensed the youth. So, in a fit of anger, he performed his salmon-leap, crossing the span in two gigantic strides, before the bridge could rise up against him. Then he strode on to Scáthach's stronghold, where he beat upon the door so fiercely that it splintered beneath his fist.

'Truly,' said the female warrior, 'this newcomer appears full of fighting mettle.' Then she sent her daughter, Uathach, to greet the stranger and show him the island.

Obediently, Uathach made Cú Chulainn welcome, conversing with him throughout the afternoon. Soon, she grew fond of the handsome young hero and decided to make him her own. On the third day after his arrival, she took him aside and put her plan into action. 'You should go and seek out my mother,' advised the maid. 'At present, she is in the upper branches of the great yew tree, giving instruction to Cuar and Cett, my brothers. Use your salmon-leap and join her there. Then, place your sword between her breasts and make her grant you three wishes.'

'And what might those three wishes be?' asked Cú Chulainn lightly, thinking that she was joking.

'Firstly, that she should train you thoroughly in all her arts, so that no other warrior may match you for skill, not even a fellow student; secondly, that I should be given to you, without any question of a bride-price; and finally, that she should tell you your fortune, for she has the gift of prophecy.'

Now Cú Chulainn saw that the maid was in earnest. Immediately, he went and carried out her bidding. As a result, Uathach became his lover and Scáthach began to instruct him in the full repertoire of her skills.

Head-Hunting

MUCH ATTENTION HAS been devoted to the Celts' interest in head-hunting, partly no doubt out of ghoulish curiosity, but also because it provides us with firm evidence that some of their activities transcended national boundaries. Several Classical authors remarked on the subject with ill-concealed fascination. Strabo, for example, reported: 'There is that custom, barbarous and exotic, that is common to many of the northern tribes … that when they depart from battle they hang the heads of their enemies from the necks of their horses and, having brought them home, nail the spectacle to the entrance of their houses.'

Another Classical writer, Diodorus Siculus, went into even greater detail: 'The heads of their most illustrious enemies, they embalm in cedar oil and preserve in a chest. These they show off to strangers, solemnly maintaining that either they or one of their ancestors had refused to part with it, even when offered a large sum of money in exchange. Some of them, we are told, boast that they have refused its weight in gold, thereby displaying a barbarous sort of greatness; for not to sell the proofs of one's valour is a noble thing.'

These accounts accord well with the archaeological evidence, which has come to light at Entremont and Roquepertuse, two Celtic shrines in southern France. Careful reconstruction has shown that severed heads were ritually displayed in these environments. They were nailed into a series of hollow niches, set in a range of porticoes. Fragments of a spearhead have been found in one of the skulls, reinforcing the argument that these were the heads of young warriors, carried off in battle. Elsewhere, there are indications that severed heads were placed on poles outside a stronghold, or offered up at the shrine of a god. In some instances, the skulls themselves were actually used as cult vessels. Livy records how the Boii, a Celtic tribe from northern Italy, cleaned out the head of a Roman general, gilded it, and then used it in their rites.

Bronze brooch of a warrior *This brooch may have been used as a talisman. It shows a mounted warrior carrying a severed head – an important symbol of power.*

There have been no comparable finds in Ireland, but the legends offer ample evidence of head-hunting. The Ulster cycle, in particular, features many passages where Cú Chulainn decapitates his foes and proudly displays their severed heads on the side of his chariot. All of this was governed by a complex code of honour. In one episode of the *Táin*, for example, Cú Chulainn deals his enemy a deadly blow. The victim, though mortally wounded, praises his conqueror and makes a dying request. He wishes to return to his camp to bid his sons farewell, but promises to return so that Cú Chulainn can behead him. Anecdotes of this kind emphasize that the capture of a severed head was more than an act of mere vainglory: it was a source of strength and prestige. In some cases, this power was exploited on the battlefield. Chroniclers relate how Ulster warriors would use brain-balls (brains hardened with lime) as slingshots, believing that these war-weapons were filled with the spirits of their defeated enemies.

For the Celts, the head was of immense value, because it housed the soul and could have talismanic properties. Irish, Welsh and Breton storytellers all gave accounts of 'living' heads, that could speak, eat and drink, even when they had been severed from their body. At the end of *The Destruction of Da Derga's Hostel*, for example, Conaire's head was struck from his shoulders, but it remained alive and recited a poem of thanks to a cup-bearer, who brought him some water to drink.

A TALISMAN

A Welsh tale from the *Mabinogion*, relating the story of Bran the Blessed, is even more remarkable. During a battle against the Irish, this hero was wounded in the foot by a poisoned spear. Realizing that his cause was hopeless, Bran ordered his followers to cut off his head and take it with them. They obeyed, bearing it with them on a lengthy voyage. These travels brought them to Harlech, where they remained for seven years, feasting endlessly while the birds of Rhiannon sang to them. After this, they journeyed to Penvro, where they entered an enchanted hall. This made them forget all their cares, causing them to devote the next fourscore years entirely to revelry. Throughout all this time, Bran's head did not decay; instead, it remained alive, feasting and conversing with his companions. Eventually, the head was buried at the White Mound, the site of the future Tower of London. There it acted as a talisman, protecting the island of Britain from invasion, until it was dug up by King Arthur.

A grotesque sculpture showing severed heads
There is evidence that human skulls were also offered to the gods of the Celtic world.

She taught him how to juggle nine apples in the air, hurling each in turn at approaching foes; she showed him how to balance on the point of a spear or the rim of a shield; she tutored him in the hero's scream, which could make an enemy fall dead on the spot; she taught him the thunder-feat, the cat's-feat and the rope-feat. He learned how to ride a sickle-chariot and how to catch a javelin in full flight. Most impor-tant of all, Scáthach gave Cú Chulainn her deadliest weapon, the *gae bolga*, a fearsome spear which could rip a man's innards to shreds.

While Cú Chulainn was in train-ing, Emer was having adventures of her own. A great lord from Munster arrived in the north, causing a great stir. His name was Lugaid, son of Nos, and he was a foster-brother of Cú Chulainn. Lugaid had travelled to Tara, hoping to win the hand of one of the twelve daughters of Cairbre Niafer. In this, he was disappointed, for all of the maids were betrothed. Forgall Manach came to hear of his mission, however, and decided to take advantage of it. Hurrying to Lugaid's side, he informed the chieftain that he was in luck. Cairbre Niafer's children might all have been promised, but his own daughter was fair-er and more talented than any of them. Lugaid was delighted by this news and desired to see her.

On that very same day, a bride-price was agreed and the wedding was arranged. Servants busied themselves, making the elaborate preparations, but Emer grieved openly. It made her sorrowful to know that her vow to Cú Chulainn would be broken so soon. Her despair was apparent to all and, shortly before the ceremony, Lugaid remarked upon it.

'What ails you, my child?' he enquired. 'Do I displease you so much?'

Emer then related the great mischief in her father's actions, explaining how she was already betrothed to Cú Chulainn. Anyone who came between them, she added, would bring deep dishonour upon himself. Lugaid was dis-turbed by this news, knowing only too well the extent of Cú Chulainn's anger. As quickly as he could, he made his excuses to Forgall and returned to Munster.

Meanwhile, on the Isle of Shadows, Cú Chulainn's devel-oping skills were being put to the test. A bloody conflict had broken out between Scáthach and Aife, her sister. Cú Chulainn was anxious to join the ranks of his teacher's forces, but Scáthach tried to prevent this. For, through her power of foresight, she knew that a terrible tragedy would ensue. Accordingly, she placed a strong sleeping draught in his wine, hoping that it would render him unconscious throughout the entire battle.

Fate, however, was not to be cheated. Such was the strength of the Irishman that he shook off the effects of the potion within an hour, though any other man would have lain unconscious for a day. Then, rising swiftly from his bed, he went out and did battle with the sons of Ilsuanach, three of Aife's fiercest champions. Within the space of thirty minutes, he put each of them to the sword and Aife's army withdrew from the field.

Next morning, the fighting began again. This time, Cú Chulainn came up against Cire, Bire and Blaicne, the three sons of Ess Enchen. As before, the confrontation was brief but bloody. Cú Chulainn wielded his sword to devastating effect and the heads of the three brothers were soon struck from their shoulders.

Now Aife herself challenged the Ulsterman, determined to put an end to his swordplay. Her reputation was mighty, for no man had ever bested her in battle, but Cú Chulainn was not dismayed. He had expected this moment and, earlier in the day, had asked Scáthach the names of the things which Aife held most dear. The question had perplexed Scáthach, but she answered truthfully that her sister's favourite possessions were her horses and chariot.

This information soon proved invaluable. Aife's skill outstripped that of the Ulster lad and it was not long before she broke his sword, leaving him nothing more than a shattered hilt. Then, as she came towards him for the kill, Cú Chulainn cried out: 'Look over there! Your horses and chariot have fallen over the cliff and are lost.' Aife hesitated for an instant and Cú Chulainn took his chance. Immediately, he hurled himself at her, knocking her to the ground. Then he pinned her beneath him, and pressed the jagged edge of his weapon close to her throat.

'Spare me, warrior,' she cried. 'Ask what you will in exchange for my life.'

'Very well, then,' said Cú Chulainn, 'I will have three wishes from you.'

'Name them in a single breath and they are yours,' she conceded.

Cú Chulainn did not hesitate. 'Firstly, you must make peace with Scáthach, giving her hostages as security. Next, you shall spend this night in my bed. Thirdly, you will bear me a son.'

'Granted. You shall have what you desire.'

And so it was. Aife's troops dispersed and went peacefully to their homes. That same night, the female warrior stayed with Cú Chulainn and, in due course, she informed him that she was expecting his child.

Cú Chulainn was delighted, confident that the baby would be a boy. Straight away, he gave Aife a golden thumb-ring, saying it was for the child. Then he made her promise that, as soon as his son was old enough to wear it, she would send him across to Ireland. In the meantime, she was to call the boy Connla and instil in him a fierce spirit of independence. 'Let him never reveal his name to a stranger,' he declared, 'or turn away from an opportunity to fight.'

Soon, it was time for Cú Chulainn to leave the Isle of Shadows and return to Ireland. As he did so, Scáthach hailed both his valour and his skill at arms. 'A glittering future lies before you, Hound of Culann. The time is coming, when you will stand alone against the forces of Cruachan. Thousands will be ranged against you, but you will scatter them with your sword and sling, reddening the earth with their blood. For thirty years, your strength and courage will set you apart, a nonpareil amongst the men of Ulster; for thirty years and maybe more, for I will not tell your future to its end. Only, be sure of this: however short your time may be, the glory of your deeds shall live for evermore.'

THE WINNING OF EMER

Cú Chulainn's safe return from the island of Scáthach was greeted with dismay by Forgall Manach. In his heart, he still cherished the hope that his daughter might be matched with Lugaid of Munster. Accordingly, he and his sons made strong their fort at Luglochta Loga and kept a close watch on Emer.

For a whole year, Cú Chulainn did not even manage to catch a glimpse of her. And, throughout this period, he did not sleep. Not from the snows of Samhain to the lambing time at Imbolc; nor from Imbolc to the day of the fires at Beltane; nor again from Beltane to Lughnasadh, when the crops were gathered in; not even in the final months, when the seasons turned again to Samhain time. And so, in this way, Cú Chulainn fulfilled the first of Emer's conditions.

At length, when the year had ended, Cú Chulainn harnessed up his sickle-chariot and drove towards Forgall's fort. There, he performed his salmon-leap, bounding over the triple-walls of its defences to reach the central enclosure. Next, he made three attacks into Forgall's stronghold. In each of these, he killed eight men, leaving a ninth to run away. And the survivors from these attacks were Scibar, Ibor and Cat, the three brothers of Emer. So, in this manner, he fulfilled the second of her conditions.

Then Cú Chulainn rescued Emer, carrying her away from her father's house. They took with them Emer's foster-sister and two wagon-loads of gold and silver. But Forgall sent men after them, pursuing them as far as Scenmend's Ford. There, they caught up with the lovers and Cú Chulainn turned to face them. In the ensuing battle, he slew one hundred men, before the couple managed to escape and continue along the river towards Emain Macha.

Soon, Forgall's men caught up with them again, this time at a place called Glondáth Ford. Once more, Cú Chulainn unsheathed his sword, reddening the earth with the blood of his foes. When the fighting subsided, one hundred of them lay dead at the river's edge.

On several more occasions, the pair were overtaken by Forgall's men and Cú Chulainn set about them with his weapons. It happened at the fords of Crúfóit, Raeban and Ath na Imfuait. In short, it happened at every ford between Ailbine and Banchuig Arcait. At each of these places Cú Chulainn slew a hundred men and, in this way, he met the last of Emer's conditions.

By nightfall, the couple reached Emain Macha, where they received a hearty welcome. There, Cú Chulainn took Emer for his wife, and all the difficulties they had faced during their long courtship were soon forgotten. After this, they remained together until they died.

THE TRAGIC DEATH OF AIFE'S ONLY SON

While Cú Chulainn was enjoying the blessings of married life, his son was growing up. During this time, Aife was mindful of her promises. Each year, on Connla's birthday, she would bring out the golden thumb-ring which the Ulsterman had left behind, and try it on the child's finger. Initially, of course, it was much too large but, on Connla's seventh birthday, it fitted perfectly. Then Aife knew that it was time to send the boy to Ireland, to seek out his father. Dutifully, she prepared Connla for the journey, giving him noble garments and weapons. She also instructed him in the *gessa*, which Cú Chulainn had specified: namely that he should never reveal his name or refuse to fight with any man who crossed his path.

Aife was not troubled by the danger that lurked in this final condition, for she and her sister had passed on their warlike skills to the young boy. In spite of his tender years therefore, Connla was more than a match for most grown men.

Some time later, the fighting men of Ulster were gathered on the beach at Trácht Éisi, when they noticed a strange craft coming towards them. It was a marvellous boat made out of bronze, with oars of shining gold. In it, there was a young lad with a pile of stones by his side. As they watched, the boy amused himself by loading the pebbles into his sling and hurling them at passing seagulls. Each shot was so accurate that the birds were merely stunned, plummeting down immediately onto the deck. The boy would then revive them, by holding them between his palms. After this, he released them and they flew up again, apparently unharmed. They did not escape, however, for the youth pursed his lips and let out a whistle, which rendered them senseless once more. Then, after cupping them in his hands for a second time, the birds rose up again. Now, having had his fun, the boy let them go, winging their way into the distance.

This spectacle alarmed the Ulstermen. 'Woe to the country which receives such a visitor,' said Conchobar, 'for if a mere lad can perform such feats, imagine the power that his elders must have! Let one of us go to meet him and prevent him from landing here.'

'Who shall go?' chorused the Ulstermen.

'Condere, son of Eochaid, is the man,' affirmed Conchobar, 'for he has no equal when it comes to fine talking and persuasiveness.'

All were agreed upon this choice, so Condere walked over and addressed the lad, just as he was beaching his boat. 'That is far enough,' he said. 'Before you land here, you must let us know the names of both your country and your family.'

The boy eyed the stranger with contempt. 'I have nothing to tell you,' he said.

'Then you must leave immediately,' countered Condere, 'for it is the law that no man may stop here, without first revealing his identity.'

'I will leave when it suits me,' answered the boy, turning away to tend to his boat.

Now Condere softened his tone. 'Very well spoken, young man. I can see you have the stuff of champions in you. But turn around, for there is no need for unpleasantness. You have come into a land of great renown. Conchobar the King will offer you his protection, and you may enjoy the society of many worthy men. Turn to me now, and I will introduce you to Amergin, the great poet; to Cethern, the red-bladed son of Fintan; and to Cumscraid, who is the leader of the mighty hosts.'

Still, the youth did not look round. 'That is a fine invitation and I thank you for it,' he said, 'but you might as well go away. Even if you had the strength of a hundred men, you would not be able to bend me to your will.'

After hearing these words, Condere went away, returning to the Ulstermen.

'That is not the way to handle such a lad,' uttered Conall the Victorious. 'Let me show you how it should be done.' So saying, he walked across to the boy and began to converse with him. 'That is a pretty talent you have with your sling,' he said, with an edge in his voice.

'It will be no less pretty, when I use it against you,' replied the youth. Then, without further ado, he took up the sling and hurled a shot at Conall. This caught him in the forehead, sending him crashing to the earth. In a daze, he tried to rise, but the lad was already upon him, binding his arms with the cord from his own shield.

'Enough,' said Conall. 'Let someone else try their luck against him.'

Hearing these words, Cú Chulainn moved towards the boy, though Emer tried to hold him back. 'That is your son,' she said, for her husband had told her of the golden thumb-ring. 'Do not go and fight with him. There is nothing brave or noble about killing your own son.'

'Silence, woman!' commanded Cú Chulainn. 'It is not your place to give me orders. The honour of Ulster compels me to challenge him, even if he is my own son.'

With these words, he went down onto the beach and approached the lad. 'I admire your games,' he said. 'You can play pretty well.'

'That is more than I can say for you,' was the reply. 'It would have been better sport if they had sent two men. A single opponent is too easy.'

'I could have brought an infant,' replied Cú Chulainn, 'for I would need no other assistance to deal with you. Come now, enough of such games. You must tell me your name or else you will die.'

'So be it,' said the lad, advancing with his sword. Then the pair exchanged blows, demonstrating all the skills that they had learned from the warrior women. Nor was the boy overwhelmed by his father. With a scything stroke from his blade, he shaved the hair from the top of Cú Chulainn's head.

'This childish mockery has gone far enough,' said the

Ulsterman, losing his patience. 'Now it is time for us to wrestle.'

'I shall not be able to reach your belt,' Connla complained, though he did not let this hinder him. With a mighty heave, he uprooted two pillar-stones and planted them in the sand. Then, mounting them swiftly, he continued to wrestle with his father. Three times he managed to duck the latter in the water, without slipping from his place. Indeed, he gripped the stones so tightly that his feet sank into them, right up to his ankles. The imprint of his feet can still be seen, and it is this which caused Trácht Éisi – the Strand of the Track – to be given its name.

After this, the wrestlers threw themselves into the sea, each one trying to drown the other. It was an even struggle and, on two occasions, Connla pulled his father's head beneath the waves. This sent Cú Chulainn into a fury and he decided to use the *gae bolga*, knowing that Scáthach had never taught its secrets to anyone else. Like a silent arrow, the spear skimmed along the surface of the water and, a moment later, Connla's bowels were spilling out onto the sea-bed.

'Alas,' cried the boy, 'I am mortally wounded. Scáthach never prepared me for that.'

'I know it,' said Cú Chulainn, and he picked up the lad and bore him out of the water. Then he carried him across to his companions. 'Here is my son, men of Ulster,' he said, and all were amazed.

Now Connla made his dying wish. 'Had I lived among you for five years,' he said, 'I would have been your champion. Many men would have fallen by my sword, and you would have had territories as far away as Rome. Since this cannot be, show me at least to the heroes who are gathered here, that I may take my leave of them.'

Connla's words were obeyed. One by one, he embraced all the Ulstermen, bidding a special farewell to his father. Then he died and a marker was set upon his grave mound. After this, the funeral feasts were held and, for the next three days, every newborn calf was slaughtered in his honour.

Celtic Decoration

THE MOST DISTINCTIVE and unifying aspect of Celtic culture is its style of decoration. This developed in the early stages of the prehistoric La Tène period, when it featured primarily on metalwork and stonework. It was still a potent force a millennium later, when illuminators came to create their magnificent manuscripts.

Simplicity and adaptability were the main reasons for this longevity. The essential components of Celtic design consisted of a few, basic shapes – spirals, interlacing, fretwork, swastikas – which were woven together to form intricate patterns. Figurative elements were sometimes combined with these abstract forms, but they were always highly stylized, echoing the rhythms of the overall design. Often, they amounted to little more than ribbon-shaped men or animals, winding round each other to create elaborate knots.

In many cases, there was a strong element of humour. The Celts were particularly fond of showing animals linked together by their tongues or tails, or humans tied together by their straggly beards. Ambiguity was another popular feature. Craftsmen delighted in using shapes which suggested bulging eyes or curving horns, teasing the viewer to find a face or animal concealed in their designs. Alternatively, they might actually include a figurative image in the design, but would then disguise it carefully, so that it could only be seen from an unusual angle. Celtic craftsmen produced infinite variations on these themes, employing them in every possible medium. As a result, a knotwork pattern on a sword might easily be reproduced on a lavish item of jewellery or a liturgical vessel.

Inevitably, styles of decoration varied considerably throughout the Celtic world. In Ireland, for example, artists were able to draw

The Turoe Stone, County Galway *A magnificent granite boulder, decorated with stylized foliage. Its four-part design may represent the four corners of the earth.*

inspiration from a number of prehistoric monuments which predated the arrival of the Celts. At Newgrange, in particular, there were swirling, spiral designs, carved into the entrance stones, which are strongly reminiscent of later Celtic patterns, but which date back to around the third millennium BC – more than two thousand years before the earliest La Tène period. Again, local craftsmen benefited from their comparative isolation. Ireland was never occupied by Rome's forces and, as a result, its artistic traditions did not become absorbed into the culture of the Empire – a fate which befell many other parts of Celtic Europe.

The extraordinary quality of the Irish La Tène style can be witnessed on a number of carved, ritual stones – most notably the one at Turoe, in County Galway – and on the golden artefacts found in the Broighter hoard. The latter was discovered in a salt-marsh by the edge of Lough Foyle, where it was probably deposited as an offering to the sea-god, Manannán Mac Lir. The hoard includes tiny models of a boat and cauldron, both of which were attributes of the god, and a magnificent, tubular collar. Its curvilinear motif is thought to represent a sea horse, another of Manannán's symbols.

THE TARA BROOCH

The items in the Broighter hoard date from around the first century BC, but the most celebrated examples of Irish design were produced several centuries later. Foremost among these was the Tara Brooch, perhaps the single most famous piece of Celtic jewellery. Its unusual shape, combining a broad hoop with an elaborate swivelling pin, was found almost exclusively in Britain and Ireland, though no other brooch can boast such exquisite detail. Crammed into its tiny space is a dazzling range of silver and gold metalworking techniques, including casting, enamelling, engraving, chip carving and filigree. The craftsman created a miniature network of interlacing, interspersed with the jaws and tails of fabulous animals and using amber and glass ornaments.

The decoration on the Tara Brooch is often compared with the designs in the Lindisfarne Gospels,

one of the most lavish Celtic manuscripts. This underlines the flexibility of La Tène decoration. Because the motifs were largely abstract, making no direct reference to the pagan beliefs of the Celts, it was relatively easy for craftsmen to adapt them to the needs of Christian patrons. In Ireland, this helped to prolong the life of the Celtic style until the early medieval period. Most of the masterpieces produced during this final phase were linked with the expansion of the Church. In addition to the manuscripts, they consisted mainly of ecclesiastical vessels, such as the Ardagh chalice, and a striking range of Celtic crosses.

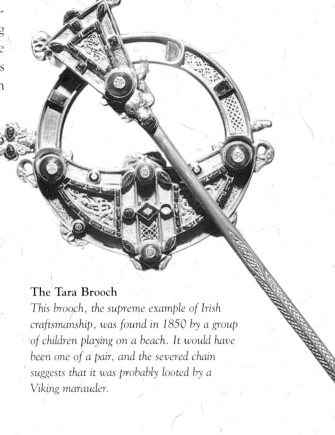

The Tara Brooch
This brooch, the supreme example of Irish craftsmanship, was found in 1850 by a group of children playing on a beach. It would have been one of a pair, and the severed chain suggests that it was probably looted by a Viking marauder.

THE ONLY JEALOUSY OF EMER

Every year, the men of Ulster held a festival on the plain of Muirthemne. For three days before Samhain and three days after it, they gathered there to enjoy all manner of feasting, drinking and sport. Such was the popularity of this event that it became renowned throughout the whole of Ireland.

It was the custom at this festival for warriors to give account of the various deeds and exploits which they had carried out over the preceding twelvemonth. Some would carry pouches where they kept the tips of tongues, cut from the mouths of their enemies. Trophies such as these were proudly displayed. It was the custom, too, for each man to place his sword over his thighs when he spoke. For, through the wonders of Samhain time, the blade would turn against its owner if he lied, or tried to pass off an animal tongue as human.

At one festival, the start of the proceedings was delayed, as the men of Ulster awaited the arrival of two of their most noble figures: Fergus Mac Roth and Conall the Victorious. During this time, they amused themselves by playing at chess, listening to the singing of the druids, and watching the jugglers perform their tricks. While they were thus engaged, a flock of birds came down and settled on a nearby lake. No other birds had ever seemed as beautiful as these, such was the magnificence of their plumage and the grace of their movements. Immediately, the women of Ulster were filled with a great longing to possess them, entreating their husbands to go and snare a couple.

'How I wish that I might have a pair of them,' said Conchobar's wife, 'for I should like to have one perching on each shoulder.'

'So would we all,' chorused the other women.

'If anyone should have such a gift, it should be me,' said Emer, 'for no one can match my husband's skill at catching birds.'

'That is true,' agreed Leborcham. 'Let me go and find Cú Chulainn right now.'

With this, she went off in search of the young hero, soon tracking him down in another part of the fairground. 'I bring a message from your wife,' she said, 'asking if you would snare some of those birds for the women of Ulster.'

Cú Chulainn reacted impatiently. 'Can't they get somebody else to do it?' he snapped.

'That kind of talk is unworthy of you,' said Leborcham. 'Remember that many of them are suffering from the third blemish on your account.'

This much was true. For the women of Ulster were afflicted with three different kinds of blemish. Those who loved Conall the Victorious had a crooked walk; those who loved Cuscraid Menn suffered the blemish of stammering; while Cú Chulainn's admirers were blind in one eye. In this, they imitated the hero himself. For, when his battle-rage was upon him, Cú Chulainn's face became horribly distorted. One eye sank back so far inside his skull that a crane's beak could not reach it, while the other bulged out like one of the massive cauldrons, used for cooking a whole calf.

'Very well, then,' he said and, calling for his charioteer, he set off towards the lake. There, he threw his sword with such unerring accuracy that many of the birds were stunned, flapping their wings helplessly as they dropped by the water's edge. Cú Chulainn continued in this way for some time, until he had amassed a considerable haul.

Then he took the beautiful creatures back to the fair, and distributed them among the women of Ulster. Such was the size of his catch, that each of them went home with a pair of birds that night. Emer alone had none.

'Are you angry?' he asked her.

'Not at all,' Emer replied, 'for I have something precious which they lack. Each of those women admires you and would have a share of you, but I have you all to myself.'

'That is nobly and elegantly said,' declared Cú Chulainn, 'and I promise you now that, if a similar flock comes again to Muirthemne, you shall have the finest of them.'

Several days later, an opportunity presented itself to the Ulsterman to make good these words. For, while he was out walking with his wife and some companions, he witnessed two beautiful birds, flying low over the lake. They were linked together by a chain of burnished gold and they sang a plaintive song, which cast a stillness over all who heard it. Immediately, Cú Chulainn took out his sling, ready to fulfil his promise. But Emer held him back.

'No, my love. Do not hurl a stone at those birds, for I sense there is something special about them. You may bring me a present some other time.'

'That cannot be,' cried Cú Chulainn. 'A promise is a promise.' With this, he loosed off a shot at one of the birds. It missed, however, and the stone fell into the water. Then he fired off a second stone but this, too, missed its mark. 'What on earth is the matter?' he moaned. 'Since the very first day that I took up arms, I have never missed such an easy target.' In his anger, he picked up his spear and hurled it at the creatures. This time, he pierced the wing of one of the birds. Together with its mate, it went down into the water and vanished from sight.

After this, Cú Chulainn strode quickly away from the lake. Feelings of anger and guilt weighed heavily on his mind. Then he sat down, resting his back against a pillar-stone. All at once, he was overcome with tiredness and fell into a deep sleep.

In his dreams, he saw two women coming towards him, one of them dressed in green and the other in purple. At first, they just laughed at him. Then they took up a pair of horsewhips and began beating him savagely. They continued in this manner for some time, until Cú Chulainn was on the brink of death. Then they turned their backs on him and walked away.

The men of Ulster could see that Cú Chulainn was suffering in his dreams, and wanted to rouse him. 'No!' said Fergus. 'You must not do that, for he is in the grip of some vision.' Eventually, the Ulsterman came out of his trance and awoke, but

he was perilously weak and had lost the power of speech. So they carried him to Tete Brecc and put him to bed. He remained there for a full year, without uttering a single word.

At last, when the seasons had gone round to Samhain time, Cú Chulainn began to stir. In a faltering voice, he told the Ulstermen of his strange vision and the pain it had caused him. They wondered at his curious story, but could find no explanation for it.

Then Conchobar made a suggestion: 'Let us take him back to the pillar-stone, where he had his vision last year. Perhaps this may help to bring about a cure.' So they returned with Cú Chulainn to the lake, and laid him by the stone. Almost immediately, he saw a woman in a green mantle coming towards him, the very one who had featured in his dream.

'It is good to see you, my lord,' she said.

'There's nothing good about it, as far as I'm concerned,' he replied. 'Why did you give me such injuries on our last meeting?'

'We did not intend to harm you,' said the woman. 'Rather, we sought to win your friendship. My name is Lí Ban and my sister is Fand. It is on her account that I am here today. Her husband, Manannán Mac Lir, has abandoned her and, in his absence, three Fomorian chieftains have risen up against her, meaning to carry her away with them. Because of this, she craves your protection and makes you this promise. In return for one day's fighting against her enemies – Senach Siaborthe, Eochaid Iuil and Eoghan Inber – she pledges to become your lover.'

'I am hardly in a fit state for fighting,' replied Cú Chulainn.

'Your weakness will soon pass,' said Lí Ban. 'My husband, Labraid, will arrange this, for he has the power to rekindle a warrior's strength.'

'Where does he dwell?' enquired the Ulsterman.

'At Mag Mell, the Plain of Delights,' answered Lí Ban. 'Come, I will take you there.'

With this, they departed for the fairy mound, where the two sisters had their home. Cú Chulainn had never seen such marvels. By the west door of the palace, there was an enormous enclosure, where magnificent herds of horses ran freely. Some were dappled grey, some were reddish-brown, and some were a fiery crimson. At the east door, there were three trees of purple glass and, concealed amid their branches, flocks of birds sang lullabies for the royal children. Then, inside the courtyard, there were thrice fifty trees, the branches of which were heavy with golden fruit, which was always ripe. And the food from these trees was sufficient to feed three hundred people. Not far beyond, there was a cauldron, full to the brim with honey wine, and the drink from this cauldron never ran dry. Finally, there was a great stone hall, lit by the brilliance of a single jewel. Thrice fifty maidens waited here, each apparelled in a splendid cloak fastened with a brooch of gold, and at their centre sat Labraid.

'Welcome, valiant warrior,' he said. 'I am pleased that you have come.'

Cú Chulainn bowed politely. 'What would you have me do?' he asked.

'First, we should inspect the troops,' said Labraid, bringing the Ulsterman to the head of his army. Cú Chulainn was amazed at their numbers, for he had never before seen so many men gathered in a single place. Then Labraid departed, leaving him alone with the warriors. As he did so, two ravens began to croak loudly, revealing druidic secrets to the army. 'This is the man of fury from Ireland,' they cawed, but the warriors just laughed at them, chasing them from the field.

Next morning, as he had promised, Cú Chulainn prepared to confront Fand's enemies. On the way, he noticed Eochaid Iuil on his way to the spring to bathe. Swiftly, he hurled his spear, wounding the man fatally. After this, Cú Chulainn's battle-rage burned fiercely. He slew thirty-three men in a single charge, before coming up against Senach Siaborthe. Their struggle was long and hard but, in the end, the Hound of Culann triumphed, taking the man's head as his trophy.

Now Cú Chulainn's charioteer, Laeg, became apprehensive. Turning to Labraid, he said: 'I fear for our safety, my lord, for my master's battle-fury is upon him and these foes are presenting little challenge. Let vats of ice-cold water be brought to cool his ardour, or he may turn his anger on us.'

Labraid followed Laeg's suggestion and three large vats were fetched. When Cú Chulainn stepped into the first, the water boiled over and spilled out of the vessel. When he entered the next one, the liquid turned into thick clouds of steam, scalding any man who was standing nearby. It was only when Cú Chulainn moved into the final vat that he began to cool down, heating the water to a gentle, simmering pitch.

Now that the battle was over, Cú Chulainn returned to Mag Mell and claimed his prize. He spent that night in Fand's bed and stayed with her for a full month. At the end of that time, he decided to return home.

Fand was sorry to see him leave. 'Tell me,' she said, 'where can we meet? For I could not bear to lose you forever.' So they made a tryst, and the place they chose was Iubar Cinn Trachta, known to many as the Strand of the Yew-Tree's Head.

Not long afterwards, the lovers kept their rendezvous, meeting under the branches of the ancient yew tree. But word of their meeting reached Emer's ears. She came too, bringing with her thrice fifty women, all armed with sharpened knives, ready to despatch the fairy woman.

Cú Chulainn stood between them. 'Have no fear,' he told Fand. 'Climb into my chariot and I will protect you. Even if all the women of Ulster were to come against us, I would make sure that you came to no harm.'

Hearing these words, Emer's anger turned to tears. 'Why do you treat me thus, my lord? Why do you shame me in front of all this company?'

But Cú Chulainn was unrepentant. 'This lady is most fair, most pure, most bright. She is well versed in all the arts, a fit mate for a king. Why should I not remain with her?'

'In truth, my lord,' countered Emer, 'this lady is no fairer than I. Things that are new and bright seem most desirable; things that are familiar seem stale. Men worship what they lack and cast aside what they already own. Oh Cú Chulainn, we were so happy once, living together in our honourable way! I wish that I could find such favour in your eyes again.'

These words softened the Ulsterman's heart. 'By my troth, you do find favour and you always shall, for as long as I draw breath.'

'Desert me, then!' cried Fand, seeing how the tables were turned.

'No,' said Emer, 'it is I who should depart.' And the two women grieved together, competing with each other in their woes.

Eventually, Manannán Mac Lir heard of this dilemma and he came to Fand. 'What will you do, wife? Will you come with me or will you wait for Cú Chulainn?'

'Truly,' she said, 'either one of you would make a fitting mate, for there is little to choose between you. I will not wait for Cú Chulainn, however, since he has betrayed me. Besides, you have no consort who is worthy of you, while he has Emer.'

But, when Cú Chulainn saw Fand depart, his heart was heavy. He leapt high in the air and, with three mighty strides, he fled to Tara Luachra. There, he lived a solitary life for many months, scarcely eating and drinking, and sleeping alone on the rough mountain road.

At last, Emer went to Emain Macha, to seek the help of King Conchobar. He sent his druids to bind

Cú Chulainn and bring him back to his home. At first, the Ulsterman resisted, threatening to kill the holy men. But the druids chanted their spells and their fairy songs, which soothed his spirits and gave him a raging thirst. Then, when Cú Chulainn begged them for a drink, they handed him a draught of forgetfulness, to wash away all memories of Fand. They gave the same potion to Emer, to cure her of her jealousy and restore her peace of mind. And Manannán Mac Lir shook his cloak between Cú Chulainn and Fand, to ensure that their paths should never cross again.

The Exile of the Sons of Usnach

It happened once that the men of Ulster were drinking in the house of Fedlimid, son of Dall. Up and down the table went the drinking horns and the feasting bowl, as the revellers filled the hall with drunken shouting. Fedlimid's wife waited upon the men, even though she was with child. Then, when they had finally drunk themselves into a stupor, she retired to her chamber.

As she walked through the room, however, the child in her womb began to shriek. So piercing was its cry that all the household was roused from its slumbers. Even the guards in the outer courtyard heard the noise and rushed inside to investigate. Then, amid all the hubbub, Sencha, the son of Ailill, called out for calm.

'Peace, my friends,' he said. 'Let the woman be brought before us and we shall see what is amiss.'

Obediently, Fedlimid's wife came before them, but she could offer no explanation for the child's behaviour. Instead, she turned to Cathbad the Druid, and asked him if he understood the meaning of the incident.

Cathbad then laid his hand upon the woman's stomach and felt the child move beneath his touch.

Celtic Magic

MAGIC AND THE SUPERNATURAL played a major role in early Celtic literature, moulding the destinies of many of its leading characters. The figures in the myths took these things for granted, showing little surprise when the fairy people from the Sidhe came to practise their arts in the world of men.

Shape-shifting was the most common form of magic. The gods could assume a variety of guises and, in many cases, were capable of inflicting similar changes upon mortals. Usually, the transformations involved animals, although other variations were possible. Thus, the Morrigán assumed the shapes of a huge black eel, a grey she-wolf, and a hornless red heifer when she did battle against Cú Chulainn. Then, when she wished him to heal her wounds, she adopted the guise of a pitiful, crippled hag. In a similar way, Rucht and Friuch took on a bewildering variety of forms in *The Contest of the Pig-Keepers*, when they were conducting their long-running feud.

The Celts' fascination with shape-shifting was probably a reflection of their interest in nature worship. The absence of written records makes this hard to define with any certainty, but many cult images have survived, showing figures that are half-human and half-animal. Carvings of the fertility god, Cernunnos, who was often depicted with antlers and a horned snake, are among the few examples to have been identified, while the

Bronze cauldron
The Dagda owned a huge magic cauldron of abundance, capable of restoring heroes to life.

meaning of many others remains a mystery. At Bouray, in France, for instance, archaeologists found a bronze statue which combines a human head with the feet of a deer. Similarly, at Euffigneix, they unearthed a stone figurine, which is part-man and part-boar.

THE DRUIDS

In many of the Irish legends, shape-shifting transformations were carried out with the aid of a druid rod or wand. This is a late addition to the myths, introduced by Christian copyists, who used the word 'druid' as a synonym for magic. The original practices of the druids, however, were far more complex. Their insistence on secrecy has obscured information about many of their activities, but it is clear that they played a major role in early Celtic society. In addition to their religious functions, they were judges, teachers and counsellors. Even the high king had to yield to their authority.

According to Caesar, druidic teaching originated in Britain, spreading subsequently to the continent. One of its main features was a belief in the transmigration of the soul, which helps to explain why Celtic warriors showed so little fear of death. Along with other Classical authors, Caesar also dwelt at length on the gory question of sacrifice. The druids certainly examined the innards of sacrificial animals when divining, but the accounts of human sacrifices being burned alive in huge, wickerwork images are rather more questionable. Instead, it is more likely that they practised divination by observing the heavens. One of the few druidic objects to have survived is the Coligny tablet, a huge bronze calendar dating from the first century BC, which lists sixty-two consecutive months covering a five-year period. On certain sections of this calendar, the words *mat* (good) and *anm* (not good) were inscribed, apparently indicating the times of the month which were most auspicious for undertaking certain actions. This corresponds with a number of passages in the Ulster cycle, where Medb consults her druids before planning the next stage of her campaign.

Magical Vessels

If the druid rod cannot be regarded as a genuine item of Celtic magic, the cauldron may make a better contender. Archaeological evidence has revealed that these were widely employed as ritual objects by the ancient Celts, figuring in ceremonial feasts and certain funeral rites. Their importance is echoed in the legends, many of which tell of cauldrons that can hold inexhaustible supplies of food. Some of these belonged to deities like the Dagda, while others could be found in magical places, such as Tir na nÓg and the Otherworld hostels.

Cauldrons were also associated with death and regeneration. The most celebrated of these vessels was owned by Bran the Blessed, a superhuman figure of Welsh legend. Any dead warriors that were cooked overnight in his cauldron were restored to life, though they lost the power of speech in the process. This legend is particularly interesting, as it seems to have parallels in the visual arts. For, one of the scenes on the Gundestrup Cauldron – the finest surviving example from the Celtic world – depicts a dead soldier being lowered into just such a vessel.

Sandstone carving of a boar-god
This carving may depict the supernatural ability of shape-shifting, in which the Celtic gods indulged.

'It was a baby girl, who uttered that terrible scream,' he said at last, 'a maid who shall bring great delight to all who look on her. Her hair will be long and golden; her eyes as blue as the brightest sky; her cheeks the tint of a foxglove in full bloom; her skin as pale as falling snow; and her lips as red as the finest coral. Many kings will compete for her favours, and many warriors will offer up their lives for love of her. Deirdre shall be her name and Ulster shall have none to compare with her.'

Cathbad's words soothed the fears of the company, but the pleasure of the Ulstermen soon turned to despair. A few days later, Fedlimid's wife gave birth to a baby girl, just as the druid had predicted. Now, however, his reaction was far less encouraging.

'Unhappy Deirdre, source of many woes! Before you have drawn your final breath, you will bring shame and ruin upon your native land. All Ulster shall bewail your dreadful deeds. Because of you, the noble sons of Usnach will suffer shameful banishment; because of you, mighty Fergus will flee from our cause and lend his strength to a foreign lord; because of you, there will be many grieving widows in Ulster.'

This prophecy caused great alarm in Fedlimid's household, and many of his entourage called for the child to be slain. But King Conchobar would not allow this. Instead, he gave orders that the child should be brought to his palace in the morning. There he would make arrangements for her upbringing and, in time, he would make her his bride. In this way, he felt sure that he could prevent the terrible fate which Cathbad had predicted.

No one dared to question Conchobar's decision and so his orders were obeyed. Deirdre was raised in his household and, as the years went by, she grew into the fairest maid in Ireland. Indeed, such was her beauty that the king placed her in a separate building, so that no man should set eyes on her, before the two of them were joined together. As a result, the only people Deirdre saw were her foster-parents and Leborcham, a female satirist who could not be kept away.

One winter's day, Leborcham was conversing with the maid, when they spied her foster-father skinning a calf outside. It was a messy job and the animal's blood flowed freely on the snow. Immediately, a raven alighted and began to drink the blood. At this moment, Deirdre turned to her companion and said:

'I could only love a man with those three colours. His hair must be as black as that raven, his cheeks must be as ruddy as the calf's blood, and his skin should be as white as snow.'

'Then you are blessed with good fortune,' replied Leborcham, 'for such a man is not far away. Naoise, son of Usnach, is his name and he lives nearby, in Emain Macha.'

'May sickness strike me down, if I do not meet him soon,' said Deirdre eagerly.

Her opportunity was not long coming. One day, Naoise was walking outside Emain's walls, singing to himself. His voice was clear and melodious, as were those of all the sons of Usnach. Every cow that heard their song produced an extra measure of milk, and every man became filled with joy and pleasure. Nor was singing their only virtue. Few warriors in Ulster were their equal in strength and courage, and few huntsmen could match them for speed and skill.

When she heard the singing, Deirdre took her chance. Slipping away from her home, she strolled past the solitary warrior. Naoise saw her, but did not know who she was.

'What fine-looking heifers they have round here,' he called out jestingly.

'The heifers are bound to be fine, in a place where there are no bulls,' she countered.

Now Naoise recognized her. 'You have as your mate the mightiest bull in the entire province: King Conchobar of Ulster.'

'If I could choose for myself,' said Deirdre, 'I would prefer a younger bull; one like yourself.'

Naoise shook his head. 'That cannot be, for I fear the prophecy of Cathbad.'

'Is that your only excuse?' she asked.

'It's a good enough one,' Naoise replied, but the girl had already leapt on him, gripping his ears. 'These two ears will be your shame and mockery, unless you take me away with you,' she laughed.

'Release me, woman,' he demanded.

'It's too late for that,' replied Deirdre, with a certainty that made him shiver.

Then Naoise began to sing out loudly, and the sound of his voice brought his brothers rushing to his side. 'What on earth are you doing?' they cried. 'If you are not careful, you will stir up trouble between us and the men of Ulster.'

Naoise explained how the maid had claimed him, and his brothers' expressions grew as dark as stormclouds. 'No good will come of this,' they said, 'but we will do our best to help you. Let us flee with her to another land, for no king in Ireland will dare to turn us away.' Naoise agreed to this and the brothers departed that night, taking their followers with them. These numbered thrice fifty warriors and thrice fifty women.

Little did the sons of Usnach know the trouble that Deirdre would bring them. For many months, they wandered through the provinces of Ireland, taking refuge wherever they could. Sometimes they joined the service of a local chieftain, and sometimes they merely hid. But, no matter where they travelled, Conchobar sought them out and tried to kill them. Eventually, they journeyed overseas to Alba, hoping to find better fortune among its wild chasms and moorlands. Here, they tried their luck as cattle thieves, making frequent raids upon the herds of Alba's farmers. Then, when this became too dangerous, they took shelter with the king of Alba, serving as soldiers under his command. For a

time, it seemed as if this might provide them with a permanent haven. Accordingly, the brothers built a house where they concealed Deirdre, fearing that she might be the cause of further mischief, if the men of Alba were to set eyes upon her.

Early one morning however, when the king's steward was walking past this house, he spied Deirdre and Naoise sleeping together. Immediately, he hurried back to his master. 'Sire,' he said, 'for many months, we have been searching in vain for a wife who is worthy of you. Now, at last, I have seen the ideal woman, living in the house of Naoise. Give me the word and I will have him slain, so that she may become your bride.'

'That you may not do,' said the king, shaking his head. 'Instead, go to her in secret and woo her on my behalf.'

The steward obeyed. Each day, when Naoise was absent, he went to speak with Deirdre, offering her sweet words and promises from his royal master. All to no avail. For, however honeyed his phrases, Deirdre simply repeated them all to Naoise. Undeterred, the king decided to send Naoise and his brothers on perilous missions, hoping that an enemy's sword might relieve him of his problem. But the sons of Usnach excelled themselves on the battlefield, destroying all who came before them.

Eventually, the king realized that Naoise could only be slain by treachery. Reluctantly, he summoned two of his guards, instructing them to kill the Irishman while he slept. Word of this reached Deirdre, however, and she warned Naoise. As a result, the brothers fled from the king's household that very night, taking the woman with them. Once more, a life of aimless wandering beckoned.

News of their plight soon reached the ears of the Ulstermen. 'It is a great shame,' they said to Conchobar, 'that our countrymen should languish so, all for the sake of an evil woman. Surely, it would be better to allow them to return home, rather than to perish at the hands of our enemies.'

'I can see your point,' agreed Conchobar. 'Inform them that they may return to Ulster, and offer them men from my household as guarantees of my protection.'

This message was warmly received by the sons of Usnach. They accepted immediately, asking for Fergus, Dubhthach and Cormac to be sent as their guarantors. Conchobar consented to this, adding just one condition. As a mark of friendship and reconciliation, he asked that the brothers should allow no morsel of food to pass their lips until they had reached his feasting table. There, he would show them the fullest measure of his hospitality.

So it was that the sons of Usnach came home to Ireland, grateful that their ordeal was over. The journey was a lengthy one but, such was their joy, they scarcely felt the pangs of hunger. It was only when they arrived at Fergus's home and saw a meal laid out before them that their stomachs began to feel their need. 'We will go on ahead,' they uttered to their three protectors, 'for we cannot wait to taste the bounties of Conchobar's table.' The others agreed and the brothers departed, accompanied only by Fergus's son.

Some time later, the walls of Emain Macha came into view. Eagerly, the brothers hurried towards them, anxious to satisfy their hunger. But, as they drew nearer, they found that Eoghan, the son of Durthacht, was waiting for them, together with his band of mercenaries. Conchobar had placed them there, with orders to prevent the trio from reaching his presence.

Eoghan wasted no time. With a mighty thrust of his spear, he stabbed Naoise, sending him reeling to the ground. Fergus's son leapt to his aid, trying to shield the stricken warrior with his own body, but Eoghan was merciless. Again and again, he plunged his weapon through the pair, until both of them lay dead. Now the brothers of Naoise drew out their swords, reddening the earth with the blood of their foes. They and their followers fought well, but Eoghan's force was too large and it was not long before they shared Naoise's fate. When the fighting was over, Deirdre was taken to Conchobar, with her hands bound behind her back.

It did not take long for reports of these terrible deeds to reach Fergus and the other guarantors. They were outraged at the way they had been used as unwitting dupes, and swore to avenge the men who had been under their protection. Because of this, much blood was spilled in the fields outside Emain. Dubhthach slew Mane and Fiachna, both kinsmen of Conchobar, while Fergus struck down Traigthren and his brother. In all, three hundred sons of Ulster laid down their lives that day. At the end of it, Fergus set fire to Emain, before he and his companions went away into exile. Together with their followers, they travelled to the land of Connacht, where they were given shelter by Medb and Ailill. Three thousand was the number of the exiles and, during the next sixteen years, their vicious raids were to bring fear and trembling into the hearts of many an Ulsterman.

Deirdre, meanwhile, remained in Conchobar's household. For a full year after Naoise's death, she did not smile or laugh; she ate no more than was necessary to survive; and her gaze was always downcast. The king sent musicians and entertainers to her, hoping to lighten her mood, but Deirdre dismissed them contemptuously.

'The sound of your pipes may be pleasant,' she would tell them, 'but I have heard far sweeter music. No songster here can produce the melodious strains that used to flow from my dear Naoise. He lies within his grave and I must weep. No more can I sleep in peace; no more do I stain my nails with pink and take delight in human company; no more can I enjoy the trappings of wealth, the touch of silken garments, or any of the fine adornments of Emain Macha. To me, this place is hateful now.'

'And the people in it?' asked Conchobar. 'Do you hate them too?'

Deirdre nodded. 'Above all,' she said, 'I hate you and Eoghan.'

Conchobar's patience snapped. 'Very well, then. You shall go to Eoghan and live with him for this next year.'

And so the king's command was carried out. Conchobar's servants took the woman away and delivered her to Eoghan. He made her sit behind him on his chariot, binding her hands so that she could not escape. For Deirdre, the very presence of the man who had killed her lover was more than she could bear.

So, one morning, as they were riding towards Emain, she threw herself from the chariot and struck her head on a boulder. Her skull split open and she died. Friends carried her body away and buried her close to Naoise. Above her grave, a pine tree began to sprout, matching the sapling on her lover's tomb. In time, these grew into mighty trees and their branches intertwined. In death, as in life, Deirdre and Naoise could not be parted.

The Cattle Raid of Cooley

The treachery of Conchobar was to bring great trouble on the men of Ulster. For, without the support of Fergus and his three thousand followers, the forces of the province were sorely weakened. Never was this loss more crucial than during the cattle raid of Cooley, when the whole of Ulster came under threat.

The conflict arose out of a quarrel between Medb, the queen of Connacht, and her husband Ailill, in which the king claimed that Medb's riches had been as naught before she married him. They agreed to compare their wealth and decide, once and for all, who was richer. The inventory began.

First, they compared their lowlier possessions: their drinking vessels, their vats and all their household goods. These were found to be equal. Next, they brought out their jewels and finery. Here, too, no difference could be found between their respective fortunes.

Then came the turn of their beasts; their flocks of sheep, their horses and pigs. Once again, they were equal. Finally, the last comparison of all was made between their herds of cattle.

These, too, were similar, except in one crucial respect. For, among Medb's herds, there had been a massive bull, which people called Fionnbanach or 'the White-Horned'. This bull, however, had thought it unseemly to be under the control of a woman and had thus joined the herds of Ailill.

When Medb realized this, she was furious. For it was plain that this was the best bull in the whole of Connacht, and she had nothing in her herd to match it. Now, all her wealth counted for nothing. She placed no value on it, if it could not equal that of her husband.

Swiftly, Medb summoned her herald, Mac Roth, and asked him to find out if there was any bull in Ireland that could compare with the White-Horned one. 'I can tell you that straight away,' answered Mac Roth. 'In Ulster, in the district of Cooley, Dáire, the son of Fachna, owns a Brown Bull that is twice as good as this one.'

'Go quickly, then,' Medb ordered, 'and ask Dáire if I can borrow his bull for a year. Tell him I will reward him well. His pay-

ment for the loan shall be fifty heifers, a fine stretch of land, a chariot to the value of thrice seven serving-maids and, most of all, my intimate friendship.'

Mac Roth obeyed, hurrying to Cooley to make the offer. It was well received. Indeed, Dáire was so pleased with the bargain that he agreed to let the bull be taken away that very day. Then, before Mac Roth and his company departed, they were shown great hospitality. Soon, many of them were drunk and, in their cups, they spoke with greater freedom.

'The owner of this house is a good man,' said one of Mac Roth's messengers. 'Do you not think it strange,' he continued, 'that he willingly gave us a prize, which the fighting men of the four provinces of Ireland would have struggled to seize?'

'There's nothing odd in that,' replied a second, 'for if Dáire had refused to hand over the bull, Medb and Ailill would have taken it by force.'

Now Dáire's steward was passing and overheard these words. Immediately, he reported them to his master and Dáire turned red with anger. 'By the gods,' he roared, 'we'll soon find out if that is true.'

Nothing more was said until the morning when the messengers came to ask Dáire where he kept the bull. He refused point blank, adding that they were lucky to be leaving Cooley with their lives. The herald could not move him on this and was forced to return to Cruachan empty-handed. Medb was angry at the failure of the mission and demanded to know the reasons. Then, when Mac Roth had explained all, she made a resolution.

'So be it! If Dáire believes that I would take the bull by force, he shall soon discover the truth of his words. Taken it shall be!'

The war which followed was to provide the showcase for Cú Chulainn's greatest exploits. At no other time was there a greater test of his superhuman courage; at no other time did his sword cut such a swathe through enemy ranks. For generations afterwards, poets and bards would sing his praises, recounting his adventures with pride and relish. It was not always so. Legend has it that some of the tales were lost, as memories of Cú Chulainn's feats receded into the past. Then by a happy chance, a questing poet came

upon the grave of Ulster's old warhorse, Fergus Mac Roth. That evening, as a mist settled over the place, the ghost of Fergus rose up, fiery and resplendent. In the space of three days and three nights, he recited all the deeds of the Ulstermen in their entirety, giving pride of place to the cattle raid of Cooley and to its hero Cú Chulainn.

THE CONTEST OF THE PIG-KEEPERS

The Brown Bull of Cooley and the White-Horned Bull of Cruachan were no ordinary creatures. This is how they came into being.

There were once two pig-keepers called Friuch and Rucht. Friuch was in the service of Bodb of Munster, while Rucht's master was Ochall Ochne of Connacht. The two men had much in common. Their names reflected their posts – Friuch took his name from the bristles of a boar, while Rucht's resembled its grunt – and both men were well practised in the art of shape-shifting. They were also great friends. Whenever the oak mast and beech nuts in Connacht were plentiful, Friuch would bring his swine north to feed on them. Similarly, whenever the trees in Munster produced the finer crop, Rucht was made welcome in the south.

But, after a time, ill-wishers stirred up trouble between the two men. The people of Connacht argued that Rucht's powers were the greater, while those of Munster sided with their man. Rucht raised the topic during his next stay in Munster and, soon, the pair were arguing.

'Let us put it to the test,' said Friuch. 'I will cast a spell on your pigs so that, however much they eat while they are in my province, they will remain lean and poor.'

The swineherd was as good as his word and, while his own pigs grew fat as they fed off the mast, Rucht's pigs became thin and sickly. When he drove them homewards, his countrymen jeered at the sorry state of his herd and Ochall Ochne dismissed him from his service. 'This proves nothing,' Rucht muttered to himself. 'I'll take my revenge when he next brings his herd to me.'

Sure enough, a year later, it was Friuch's turn to lead his pigs into the neighbouring province. Rucht cast a similar spell over them and the beasts remained thin, no matter how much they ate. When Friuch returned home, he too was dismissed from his post.

This did not put an end to the swineherds' quarrel. They turned themselves into ravens and made a great cawing noise, scolding each other constantly. They spent a whole year in Connacht at the fort of Cruachan, squabbling in this way. Then they flew south to Munster, to continue with their bickering. Here, they were spotted by Ochell's steward, Findell.

'What a racket those birds are making,' he exclaimed. 'They sound as bad as the two we had in Cruachan last year.' With that, the ravens turned back into men and Findell greeted them, recognizing them as the shape-shifting swineherds.

'You do wrong to welcome us,' said Friuch, 'for we shall be the cause of many deaths. Wives shall weep for husbands, sisters shall weep for brothers, all on our account.'

Findell was shocked by this gloomy prophecy and tried to discover what lay behind it, asking the pig-keepers what they had been doing since their last meeting.

'We have been up to no good,' came the reply. 'Since you last saw us, we have been living in the shape of birds, pursuing our quarrel. We have been in these forms for two years and now we plan to change again, this time into water creatures.'

Then, as Findell looked on, the two men underwent the promised transformation and slid into the water. They spent the next year in the River Siuir and the year after that in the River Sionnan, all the time attempting to devour each other.

Nor were these the final transformations of Rucht and Friuch. Next, they turned themselves into war-mongering champions, urging men into battle. Four kings died in the conflicts they caused, and Ochall and Bodb were among them. Then they became shadows, threatening each other. Many people died of fright after witnessing their phantom shapes.

At length, the pig-keepers changed themselves into eels. One of them went into the River Cruind, in the district of Cooley. There, it was swallowed up by a cow belonging to Dáire, son of Fachna. The second eel, meanwhile, slipped into the spring of Uaran Garad in Connacht. Medb saw it there one day and fished it out of the water in a small bronze vessel. She gazed at it for a long time, since it was like no eel that she had ever seen before. Many colours danced upon the surface of its skin. 'What a strange creature you are,' she whispered, 'and what a pity it is that you cannot speak to me.'

'What is it that you want to know?' the eel enquired.

Medb was astonished. 'What kind of beast are you?' she said.

'A tormented one,' the eel replied. 'I have lived in different shapes for many years and I am tired of my wanderings.' With that, it slithered out of the vessel and swam away in the water. A short time after that, it was swallowed up by a cow that came to drink at the spring.

Now the two swineherds underwent their final transformations. Rucht, who had been swallowed by Medb's cow, was reborn as the White-Horned Bull, while Friuch was calved as the Brown Bull of Cooley. And in their final shapes, the quarrelling pig-keepers led all the peoples of Ulster and Connacht into war.

MACHA'S CURSE ON ULSTER

When Medb ordered her forces to march on Cooley, she was confident of an easy victory. For, though the fierceness and courage of the Ulstermen was trumpeted throughout Ireland, she knew that they lay under a curse, which made them too weak to fight. This is how the Ulstermen came to be afflicted.

There was in Ulster a rich landowner named Crunniuc, the son of Agnoman. He lived in a remote, mountainous part of the province with his sons. His wife was dead and so he was obliged to manage the house himself. Then one day, while he was sitting there alone, an unknown woman entered the place. She was tall, finely dressed and had noble features. Crunniuc looked up at her, expecting her to say something, but the woman remained silent. Instead, she walked straight over to the hearth and began tending the fire, as if she were a serving-maid. After this, she put the household in order, prepared a meal and went out to milk the cows. That night, she slept with Crunniuc. And, in all this time, she never spoke a word.

The woman stayed on at Crunniuc's house and, some time later, she married him. She continued to manage his household, look after his sons and, in due course, she informed him that she was expecting their child. All seemed well until the day of the great festival, when the men of Ulster met to compete in races, games and other amusements. Crunniuc decided to go, since all the other men of

his standing were to be there, but his wife warned him against it. 'Do not go to the fair,' she pleaded, 'for if you so much as mention my name, I will be lost to you forever.'

'If that is the case, I shall take care that I do not speak of you at all,' Crunniuc assured her.

So saying, he set off for the fair. This proved to be just as grand an occasion as he had anticipated. The highlight occurred towards the end of the day, when the king's chariot was brought out onto the field. It won the main race with ease and the poets, the druids and the assembled crowds all joined in praise of the royal horses. 'Nothing can match the speed of these beasts,' they cried. 'There are no better runners in the whole of Ireland.'

Crunniuc scoffed at this. 'Why, my wife could run faster than them.' These foolish words were overheard and the king was informed. His wrath was fearsome. 'Take hold of the man,' he ordered, 'and keep him prisoner until his wife is brought here. She must make good his boast.'

So, the king's men held him fast and messengers were sent to his house, to fetch his wife. When she heard what her husband had done, she pleaded with the messengers: 'What he said was rash indeed, but I cannot come. As you can see, I am full with child and my time is near.'

'That would be a great pity,' said the men, 'for if you do not come with us, your husband will be put to death.'

'Then I have no choice,' she said. 'I must go with you, whatever happens.'

So, Crunniuc's wife went to the festival with the messengers, where she was brought before the king. Once more, she asked for mercy, showing him her condition. She even asked for a delay, promising to race against the royal chariot team after she had given birth to her child. But the king would brook no delay, stating that her husband would forfeit his life if she refused to run.

Then the woman turned to the people of Ulster, who were gathered there in their thousands. 'Help me,' she cried out. 'Surely, you must see my plight, for a mother bore each and every one of you. Help me, pity me. Wait until my child is born.'

Celtic Weapons

THE EARLY IRISH LEGENDS celebrated an age of heroism, so it was only natural that the leading characters should have wielded a magnificent array of weapons. Many of these had special powers, adding to their owner's air of invincibility. Cú Chulainn, for example, carried the *gae bolga*, a mighty spear which never seemed to miss its mark and which was devastatingly efficient at disembowelling his foes. Similarly, Fergus fought with a sword named *cladcholg*, which was strong enough to cut through the sides of mountains. Other items had

magical qualities. Conchobar, the king of Ulster, possessed a shield which acted as an alarm; Ochain (the 'Moaner') screamed aloud whenever it was struck, and made all the other shields in Ulster sing out with it.

The beauty and splendour of these pieces had some basis in reality. The Celts were extremely proud of their weapons and craftsmen lavished great care on their production. The finest helmets were covered in gold foil or inlaid with ivory, amber and precious stones. Sword hilts received similar treatment, while scabbards and shields were often decorated with swirling tendril patterns. Some of these items were too fragile and costly for use in battle. Instead, they were designed as sacrificial items, to be offered

Detail of the Battersea Shield
Enamelled swastikas form part of the decoration on this superb bronze shield.

up at the shrines of the gods, or else for use on ceremonial occasions. Many of the latter have come down to us from princely graves, where the warrior chieftain was invariably buried with the most dazzling symbols of his prowess. However, some ornamental elements evolved from functional needs. The Celts, for example, liked to use oblong shields with a small, circular boss in the centre, concealing the handgrip. From the start, this boss provided the main focus of the decoration. Warriors soon noted, however, that the nails which held it in place could be pushed dangerously close to the wearer's hand, if the shield was struck hard enough. Gradually, therefore, the raised section grew larger and larger, until it formed a long, rib-shaped protrusion, running the full length of the shield. On ceremonial pieces, this entire area was decorated with engraved motifs. On the Battersea shield, for example, the handgrip area was covered in extravagant curves and spirals, resembling huge eyes, bull's horns or flowing moustaches.

IRISH ARTEFACTS

In Ireland, the finest relics of military equipment come from the area around Lisnacrogher, in County Antrim. Here, archaeologists recovered seven bronze scabbard plates, along with a complete scabbard together with its iron sword. All are engraved with flowing arrangements of S-curves and spiral patterns. Most of the items were retrieved from the River Bann or from marshy ground nearby, suggesting that they were either deposited at a watery shrine or else belonged to a crannog (lake dwelling). Other notable finds include a number of sheet-metal war-trumpets. The Celts

Lisnacrogher Scabbard
Compasses were used to design the intricate leaf and spiral patterns on this early Irish scabbard.

made great use of these on the battlefield, hoping that the terrible noise would throw their enemies into confusion. Significantly, perhaps, one of the war-trumpets was found close to the site of Navan Fort, regarded by many as the original location of Emain Macha – the seat of the kings of Ulster.

METHODS OF WARFARE

The legends themselves shed further light on Irish methods of warfare. Cú Chulainn's exploits at the ford revolve around a series of single combats, which provide a showcase for his superhuman strength, stamina and technical skill. This, however, was exceptional. For most chieftains of the warrior caste, fighting was conducted in chariots. Classical authors relate how the Celts used to career around the battlefield in these, uttering fearful shrieks and hurling their spears, before descending to fight on foot. The chariots were large enough to carry two men, the soldier and the charioteer, and the latter's role was vital. He would remain close to the centre of the action, ready to rescue his master if was wounded or became exhausted. This explains the unusual status of charioteers such as Laeg, who was part-servant, part-companion and part-protector to Cú Chulainn.

Physical remains of chariots are scanty, although in some parts of the Celtic world warriors were buried with them. The practice was particularly popular in the Champagne region of France. In graves of this kind, archaeologists have uncovered a wealth of metal harness plaques, linchpins, axle rings and terrets (loops for controlling the reins). Some are decorated with stylized animals, while others have colourful enamel inlays.

But the crowd remained unmoved and urged her to race for them.

'Very well,' she said at last, 'but a great evil will come of this and it will afflict the whole of Ulster.'

'What is your name?' demanded the king.

'I am Macha, daughter of Sainrith Mac Imbath, and I promise you that my name and those of my heirs will mark this place forever.'

Then she went out to where the horses were waiting with the king's chariot. The race began and Macha outran the horses, beating them to the winning post. But the effort cost her greatly and there, at that very spot, the pains of childbirth came upon her. She screamed aloud as two children were born to her, a boy and a girl. That is why the place was later known as Emain Macha, or 'the Twins of Macha'.

In her agony, Macha placed a curse on the men of Ulster, saying that all those who heard her cries would come to know the pain she had experienced. For five days and four nights, they would suffer the same pain and weakness as a woman giving birth. And this curse would afflict all the men of Ulster and it would be passed down to their heirs. For nine generations, they would suffer in the same way, and the weakness would come upon them in the hour of their greatest need, when their enemies were closing in on them. Only three classes of people were spared from this fate. They were the young boys of Ulster, the women of Ulster and the family of the warrior Cú Chulainn.

This is the weakness that afflicted the men of Ulster, when Medb and Ailill moved their armies against them.

CÚ CHULAINN HARRIES THE ENEMY

The Connacht army encountered no resistance, when it crossed the border into Ulster. Because of Macha's curse, the men of Ulster had not the means to defend their property from Medb's marauding hordes. What is more, their advance might have continued unchecked, but for the love which Mac Roth still bore for his native land. Secretly, he sent messengers to Cú Chulainn, informing him of

the invaders' route and imploring him to hinder its progress.

Cú Chulainn's response was decisive. Without delay, he hastened to the place that Fergus had indicated, desperate to confront the enemy. He did not have long to wait. For, at a place called Athgowla, north of Knowth, he came upon the four sons of Iraird Mac Anchinne. He despatched them swiftly, severing their heads from their bodies.

Then he cut down a tree with a single stroke of his sword, lopped off all but four of its branches, and rammed the trunk into the bed of a nearby stream. On the tips of these four branches, he impaled the heads of his victims. Next, he turned their chariots around and whipped the horses, so that they would carry the evidence of his deed back to Medb and her forces.

Sure enough, the blood-smeared chariots thundered back to the Connacht people. There, the sight was greeted with alarm, for it seemed certain that some part of the army of Ulster must be lying in wait for them nearby. When they arrived at the stream, however, and saw the four heads still dripping with gore, they noticed only a single chariot track. In addition, when the tree was uprooted from the stream, it was clear that it had been felled with a single sword-stroke.

'Can one man alone have done all this?' asked Ailill, astounded.

'Indeed, he can,' replied Fergus Mac Roth. And that night, when the people of Connacht had made their camp and taken their fill of food, he told them of Cú Chulainn and of the marvellous feats that he had achieved in his brief life. In this way, the men of Connacht came to learn of the awesome prowess of the enemy that they were about to face.

Next morning, Ailill's force moved on to Mag Mucceda. There, they found an ogham message, carved on the side of a felled oak. It was a *geis*, laid by Cú Chulainn, which specified that no one could pass that place until a warrior had leapt over the trunk in his chariot. Many a warrior attempted this feat without success. In all, thirty horses were killed and thirty chariots broken, before the men of Connacht were able to continue on their way.

Now Medb sent out some of her finest warriors to scour the countryside, hoping that they might catch the Ulsterman unawares. So it was at Ath Fuait, where Fraech, the brother of Boann, found Cú Chulainn bathing in the river. 'Wait here,' he told his followers. 'I will go into the water and fight with him there, for it may be that he is weaker away from the land.' Then he took off his tunic and walked towards the river.

Cú Chulainn saw him approach. 'Come no closer,' he boomed. 'If you challenge me here, you will die for it, and I should be sorry to kill you.'

'Save your words, Hound of Ulster. You cannot escape me.'

'Very well then,' said Cú Chulainn, 'how shall we fight?'

'Let us wrestle,' answered Fraech, 'for no man can best me at that.'

So saying, he leapt at the Ulsterman and sent him tumbling. For the next few minutes, the two men threshed about wildly in the water, until Cú Chulainn managed to push his opponent's head beneath the surface. Then, a moment later, he pulled it up again. 'Surrender now and I will spare you,' said Cú Chulainn, while Fraech gasped for breath.

'Never!' was his only reply. At this, Cú Chulainn pushed Fraech under the water once more, and held him there until he was dead.

Then a troop of women in green tunics came and bore the body away to the fairy mounds, for Fraech's kinsmen were people of the Sidhe.

Not long afterwards, Cú Chulainn came across another of the enemy at a place called Tamlacht Orlaim, a little to the north of Disert Lochait. The man in question was a charioteer, who was busy mending a broken shaft. At first, Cú Chulainn thought he was an Ulsterman and he went over to reprimand him, for carrying out his task so close to the Connacht host.

'What on earth do you think you are doing?' he called out, as he approached the fellow.

'Cutting a new shaft,' replied the other. 'My chariot broke, when I was out chasing that wild deer, Cú Chulainn. Can you lend me a hand?'

'Of course. I will trim the wood for you.' And so saying, Cú Chulainn snapped off a branch from a nearby tree and began to strip it with his bare hands. The charioteer watched this feat of strength with mounting horror. 'This is not your usual work, is it?' he enquired cautiously.

Cú Chulainn smiled, as he changed the subject. 'What is your name?' he asked.

'I am the charioteer of Orlam, Ailill's son. And you, what is your name?'

'I am Cú Chulainn,' he replied.

'I feared that you might be,' said the other, dropping his paring knife in abject terror.

'Do not worry,' said Cú Chulainn, 'I'm not interested in mere charioteers. Just tell me where your master is.'

The charioteer waved his arm to the right. 'He is over there, working in that ditch.'

'Come with me, then, but keep quiet.'

The two men rose to their feet and walked silently across to the ditch. There, Cú Chulainn killed Orlam and cut off his head. Then he tied it round the charioteer's neck with a leather thong, so that the gory object was resting on his back.

'There now, take that back to your camp and show the king. Don't try to remove it, or I will split your head with a stone from my sling.'

Terrified, the charioteer did as he was told. At the camp, Medb and Ailill looked sadly upon the head of their son. 'We thought this war was going to be as simple as killing a few birds,' said the queen bitterly. 'Never did we imagine that it would cost us so dear.'

As the Connacht army moved on to Methe, Cú Chulainn continued to harass it whenever possible. Increasingly, he crept closer to the host, hoping that he might find an opportunity to kill Medb or Ailill with a shot from his sling. His accuracy was deadly. On one occasion, he slew a squirrel that was perched on Medb's shoulder; on another, he killed a bird that was eating out of Ailill's hand. Eventually, Medb became so nervous that she had a company of men walk beside her, holding their shields aloft in order to protect her from the Ulsterman.

This did not deter Cú Chulainn. Early one morning, he saw a woman who resembled Medb, walking towards the river to bathe, surrounded by a large group of other women. Swiftly, he hurled off two stones from his sling and broke her head apart. But this was not the queen. It was Lochu, one of her attendants.

The carnage increased even more when the army reached Druim Feine in Conaille. There, Cú Chulainn harried them from a distance with his sling. From his vantage point at Ochaine, he killed a hundred men on each of the three nights that the invaders rested there.

'This is hopeless,' cried Ailill. 'Our army will melt away, if we do not stem this flow of blood. Let us make a pact with him. I will offer him a portion of the plain of Ai that is equal in size to the whole of Muirthemne. In addition, he may have my finest chariot, harnessed and equipped with a dozen men. Or, if he prefers it, he may have the plain where he was raised, along with full compensation for all the cattle and household goods that we have destroyed. All he has to do in exchange is swear his allegiance to me; a small enough thing to ask, since I am a far superior master to that half-king, Conchobar.'

So Mac Roth – the herald, who could circle the whole of Ireland in just one day – was sent to bear this message to Cú Chulainn. He found him at Delga, resting after his exertions.

'I see a man coming towards us,' said Laeg to his master.

'Quickly, describe him to me,' ordered Cú Chulainn.

'He has a full head of yellow hair, wrapped with a linen band; he wears a hooded tunic and a brown cloak, fastened with a spear-shaped brooch; he carries a white hazel rod in one hand and a vicious club in the other; and at his waist, there is a sword with a sea-horse tooth for a hilt.'

'Let him come,' said Cú Chulainn, 'for these are the tokens of a herald.'

Mac Roth approached and asked the young warrior for his name.

'I am a servant of Conchobar Mac Nessa,' Cú Chulainn replied.

'Is that the best answer you can give me?'

'It will suffice.'

'Can you tell me, then, where I might find Cú Chulainn?'

'What would you say to him, if he was here?'

When he heard this, Mac Roth guessed that this imperious young man was Cú Chulainn himself and he delivered his message. But the youth continued to talk in a most disdainful manner.

'If Cú Chulainn were here, he would reject your offer. He would not trade his mother's brother for another king.'

So Mac Roth went back to Ailill, returning a short time later with a new message. The king now offered him all the noblest women and the cows without milk from the booty they had plundered. All that was asked in return was that he should stop attacking them with his sling by night, though he could do as he wished by day.

Cú Chulainn was as scornful as before. 'I will not agree. For, if you take away our serving-women, our noble ladies will be forced to do menial work, and without milch-cows we will have no milk.'

Once more, Mac Roth departed, to obtain new conditions. These were soon forthcoming. Ailill now promised Cú Chulainn all the serving-women and the milch-cows that they had seized in their raids. Still, however, the youth was not satisfied.

'I cannot agree to that,' he replied, 'for then the Ulstermen would take serving-women to their beds and would breed a race of slaves. Besides that, they would have to use the milch-cows for meat in the winter.'

'Are there any terms which would satisfy you?' the herald then enquired.

'There are,' replied Cú Chulainn, 'but you must find them out for yourself. One man in the Connacht camp will know what I mean. If you send him to me with the offer, I will accept it.'

Mac Roth returned again to his masters with this puzzling answer. They did not know what to make of it, until Fergus provided the explanation.

'I know what he has in mind,' he said, 'though it is scarcely good news for you. He will fight the men of Connacht one by one, at the ford. While the combat is in progress, your army may march on unhindered. But, as soon as he has defeated the man sent against him, it must stop and make camp until the following day. In this way, he means to delay you until the men of Ulster have recovered from their weakness.'

'Even so,' said Ailill, 'it will be far better for us to lose a single man every day, rather than a hundred every night. Go to him, Fergus, and tell him we accept his offer.'

Many heroes came to try their chance against Cú Chulainn at the ford, but none was successful. Soon, the Ulsterman's prowess had caused such a stir that the men of Connacht began to bargain with their king. Thus it was with Nadcrantail, when he was called into the presence of Ailill.

'Grant me the hand of Findabair, your daughter, and I will fight Cú Chulainn,' said the warrior. Reluctantly, Ailill bowed his head in agreement.

So, the following morning, Nadcrantail rode to the ford. With him, he took his favourite weapons, nine holly spears which had been specially charred and sharpened. Cú Chulainn, meanwhile, was busy chasing birds and paid little attention to the stranger. Even when Nadcrantail hurled a spear at him, he brushed it aside with ease and kept his eyes on the birds. The same thing happened when his opponent threw the other eight spears. The last one, however, frightened the birds, causing them to take flight. Cú Chulainn chased after them and, from a distance, it looked as if he was running away.

'Is this the great hero of Ulster before me?' sneered Nadcrantail. 'I had thought to have a better fight than this.'

'And so you should,' replied Cú Chulainn, 'if you came against me with a weapon in your hand. For I will not kill an unarmed man. Still, if you have a mind for battle, return tomorrow and we will test our strength in earnest.'

The Book of Kells

THE BOOK OF KELLS is probably the finest and most celebrated of the illuminated manuscripts, that were produced for the early Celtic Church. Although, of course, these lavish objects were primarily designed to glorify the Word of God, they were also beautiful artworks in their own right. In part, this was because they made use of ancient traditions of decoration, which Celtic craftsmen had honed to perfection over the course of many centuries.

The precise origins of the Book of Kells are shrouded in mystery. It takes its name from the monastery of Kells in County Meath, where it was lodged from an early date. Indeed, the very first documentary reference to the book describes its theft from Kells. In an entry for the year 1006–7, the chronicler of the Annals of Ulster relates how 'the chief relic of the western world was wickedly stolen during the night from the western sacristy of the great stone church of Cennanus [Kells], on account of its wrought shrine. That Gospel was found after twenty nights and two months with its gold stolen from it, buried in the ground.' In other words, the thief made off with the costly shrine, where the book was displayed, and discarded the actual manuscript.

It is possible that the book itself was produced at Kells, although most authorities regard

Decorated initial, Book of Kells
Celtic illuminators loved to use ribbon-like animals in their texts. Here, a lion and a snake coil round each other to form the letter 'R'.

the Scottish island of Iona as a more likely candidate. This was the head of a confederation of monasteries, which followed the teachings of St Columba. As such, it would have had both the manpower and the wealth that were vital for a project of this kind – the parchment alone would have necessitated the slaughter of a sizeable herd of cattle. In addition, the monks of Iona sought refuge at Kells, following a series of Viking raids which devastated their monastery. This move took place in the early years of the ninth century, the very period when the manuscript was probably being produced. These disruptions to the monks' way of life may also explain why the book was never completed.

DECORATIVE DESIGNS

The outstanding feature of the Book of Kells is its sumptuous decoration. This consists of two basic forms of design. There are figurative images – notably the portraits of the Evangelists and a few Biblical scenes – together with full-length pages of decorative, abstract patterns. The portraits were a standard feature of early Gospel Books, with some Irish examples dating back as far as the seventh century. The Biblical illustrations, however, were a radical new departure; the image of the Virgin and Child, for example, is the oldest, surviving version in a British or Irish manuscript. The trend towards figuration developed after the Synod of Whitby (664), when the Celtic Church lost some of its independent character, by agreeing to follow the dictates of the papacy. Increasingly, books were sent across from Rome and copied out in British and Irish monasteries. Over a period of time, this meant that the style of Christian manuscripts became far more eclectic.

The abstract decoration in the Book of Kells was the product of an older and more vibrant tradition. The knotwork, swirling spirals and stylized creatures derived from the designs of the Celts, a tribal people whose artistic influence extended over much of pre-Christian Europe. They used these motifs on a wide variety of objects, ranging from weapons and jewellery to general household goods and horse-trappings. Christian artists swiftly adapted these patterns, even though images of fierce beasts and humorous beard-tugging men, sometimes formed a slightly uneasy accompaniment to the message of the Gospels. For example, on the Monogram Page the artist managed to insert a pair of cats and mice nibbling communion wafers below the 'X', an otter with a fish below the 'P' and a large moth near the the top of the 'X'. Nevertheless, it is precisely these extravagant passages of decoration which have earned the Book of Kells its worldwide renown. No other manuscript can match the splendour of its elaborate lettering and initials, which weave such a hypnotic spell upon the viewer.

The irresistible appeal of the Celtic Gospel books has long been recognized. Evidence of this can be found in the oft-cited appraisal of one such manuscript by the twelfth-century

The Monogram Page, Book of Kells
Angels, cats and human heads are playfully concealed in this elaborate depiction of Christ's monogram, 'XP'.

historian, Gerald of Wales, 'Fine craftsmanship is all about you, though you may not immediately notice it. Look keenly at it, however, and you will penetrate to the very shrine of art. For, you will make out intricacies so delicate and subtle, with colours so fresh and vivid, that you might say that all this was the work of an angel, not a man.'

Nadcrantail agreed and came back the following day, carrying with him a new set of holly spears. Cú Chulainn invited him to make the first throw and his enemy took aim. The spear flew fast and true, but the Ulsterman used his salmon-leap and soared above it.

'I can do as well as that,' declared proud Nadcrantail, preparing to jump. But Cú Chulainn fooled him. He lobbed his weapon high, so that it speared through the other from above, pinning him to the ground.

'Alas,' cried Nadcrantail, 'you have bested me.' Then Cú Chulainn came close and finished him off, slicing his torso into four quarters.

Another time, Medb and Ailill tried to trick the Ulsterman. They sent Lugaid with a message, offering him the hand of Findabair, if he would leave the Connacht army alone.

'I sense a trap,' thought Cú Chulainn, but he decided to play along with it.

Ailill then put his plan into action. 'Let my fool, Tamun, dress up in my clothes and go in my place. Then he may take my daughter and pledge her to the Ulsterman. With luck, Cú Chulainn may be taken in by this and cease his attacks upon us.'

All this was done. Tamun put on Ailill's robes and placed his crown upon his head. Next, he walked up the hill, to the place where Cú Chulainn had made his camp. Then he called out to the warrior, making sure that he did not come too close to him, for fear of being recognized.

Cú Chulainn did not bother to reply. He knew from the sound of the man's voice that this was no king. Instead, he drew back his sling and hurled a stone at the fellow, taking out his brain. Then he went up to the girl and cut off her hair with his sword, placing the tresses around the top of a pillar-stone. After this, he lifted up a second pillar-stone

and rammed it through the corpse of the king's fool. These two stone monoliths are there to this day, known to all as Findabair's Pillar and the Fool's Stone.

FERGUS IS CHOSEN

Once the supreme abilities of the Ulster hero became apparent, there were few volunteers willing to fight with Cú Chulainn at the ford. At length, Medb turned to Fergus and tried to persuade him to take up the challenge. He refused stubbornly, arguing that he should never be expected to go into combat against a boy who was both his foster-son and his pupil. But Medb was persistent, plying him with wine to soften his resistance. Eventually, when he was thoroughly drunk, Fergus gave in to her entreaties and agreed to go to the ford.

The encounter took place on the following day. By this time, Fergus had devised a means of allaying his conscience. As he marched resolutely towards the ford, Cú Chulainn noticed that his opponent's scabbard was empty.

'You are a brave man, Fergus, to come against me without a sword.'

'It makes no difference; I would never use one on you. Instead, I would ask you to yield to me now, and I will return the favour at another time.'

'You will yield to me, when I ask you?'

'I give you my word,' agreed Fergus.

So Cú Chulainn gave way before him, allowing the Connacht army to advance unhindered for the space of a day. He felt no shame in this, for he knew that it would be more useful to have his foster-father yield to him on the day of the great battle.

THE DUEL AT THE FORD

The last and greatest of the challengers at the ford was Ferdia, son of Daire, the horn-skinned champion from Irrus Domnann. He and Cú Chulainn were foster-brothers and had learned their skills together on Scáthach's isle. From his memories of their early training bouts, Cú Chulainn knew only too well that this would be his toughest adversary.

Ferdia was even more apprehensive. The Hound of Culann had already performed miracles against the Connacht army. Who could be sure of keeping their head on their shoulders, when they came up against such a man? Because of this, he slept little on the eve of the duel. In the morning, he rose early and travelled to the ford shortly after daybreak. There he waited nervously, until a cloud of dust on the horizon signalled that Cú Chulainn was approaching. A shiver went down his spine as he watched the chariot draw near, its horses sweeping across the countryside like the gusting of an autumn gale.

A moment later, Cú Chulainn stepped down from the chariot and walked towards the ford. Ferdia greeted him politely and invited him to name his choice of weapons. This, the Ulsterman declined. 'No,' he said. 'You arrived first at the ford. That honour belongs to you.'

So Ferdia made his selection, opting for the casting weapons that they had used so often on Scáthach's practice field. Swiftly, they assembled these – the round-handled spears, the quill darts, the ivory-hilted daggers – and began hurling them at one another. All morning, the missiles flew between them, making a sound like bees in flight. But both warriors were so skilled at fending the spears off with their shields that no harm was done. At midday, they agreed to stop, since their weapons were all blunted, and they handed the broken darts and spears to their charioteers. In the afternoon, they switched to broader spears, bound with flaxen cord. For several hours, they hurled these at each other until both men were exhausted.

'Let us leave this now,' said Ferdia, as nightfall approached.

'Agreed,' said Cú Chulainn. 'The time is right.'

So they left off fighting, cast their spears away, and embraced each other warmly. Their horses were put in the one enclosure that night and their charioteers shared the same fire. Green rushes were laid out for them and healers came to dress their wounds. And Cú Chulainn made sure that for every plant and herb that was placed on one of his wounds, a similar one was also sent across to Ferdia, on the other side of the ford. For, if he were to defeat Ferdia, he did not want it said that his opponent died for want of proper healing. In the same way, Ferdia sent across a half-share of all the fine foods and wine that the men of Ireland had provided for him. For, if he were to slay Cú Chulainn, he did not want it said that the Hound of Culann was weak from lack of nourishment.

Next day, their battle continued. 'What weapons shall we use today?' asked Cú Chulainn.

'You must choose,' replied Ferdia, 'for I had the choice of weapon yesterday.'

'Then let us use our heavy stabbing-spears,' said Cú Chulainn, 'for that way we may bring our conflict to a close more quickly.'

So it was agreed, and from dawn till dusk they probed and pierced each other with the vicious implements. If it were the custom for birds in flight to pass through the bodies of men, they could have flown with ease through the gaping, bloody wounds left by the sharpened spear-points.

At nightfall, the two men drew apart. 'Let us stop this now, Ferdia,' said Cú Chulainn, 'for our horses are tired and our charioteers are drained.'

'You are right,' agreed Ferdia, 'we have done enough for one day.'

So the friends embraced and, as on the previous night, they shared what comforts were available to them.

Next morning, Cú Chulainn looked at his old companion and felt a pang of sorrow for all the hurts he had laid on him.

'You look weary, Ferdia,' he called out. 'There is a dullness in your eyes and a dark shadow cast about your head and shoulders.'

Once again, Cú Chulainn tried to persuade his foe to leave the ford and forget the rewards that Medb had offered. But Ferdia was determined to continue and, as it was his choice of weapons that day, he suggested that they turn to their huge, death-dealing swords.

Battle commenced and, as the sun ran its course across the sky, the two men hacked away with their blades. Broad were the lumps of flesh that they cut from each other's flanks, and crimson the blood that flowed and clotted on their wounds. When night arrived they parted, sorrowful and silent, each knowing that the end was near. Their horses did not rest in the one enclosure that night, nor did the charioteers sit by the same fire.

When morning came, Ferdia rose early, donned his finest battle gear and went to wait for Cú Chulainn. 'What arms shall we try, today?' cried the latter, as he joined him.

'The choice is yours, as you know.'

'Very well, then, let us try fighting in the river.'

'Let us, indeed,' said Ferdia. But, though he made light of it, his heart was heavy; for he knew that Cú Chulainn had defeated all who came against him in the waters of the ford. Nonetheless, the two men began to lay into each other viciously and, until midday, they matched each other blow for blow. Then, as the pace grew hotter, Cú Chulainn leapt onto the boss of Ferdia's shield and aimed a blow at his head. But the latter cast him off, tossing him onto the bank as if he weighed no more than a babe in arms.

Immediately, Cú Chulainn leapt up again, attempting the same manoeuvre. Once more, his adversary cast him away with ease. The Hound of Culann tried the ploy a further time and, when it failed, his anger came upon him. His frame swelled up grotesquely, his features dissolved into a wicked snarl, a blinding light shone from his forehead, and a cascade of boiling blood spurted from his skull. While he was gripped in this fury, he threw himself on Ferdia and grappled with him at close quarters.

Together, they thrashed about, displacing so much water from the river that there was room enough for a king and queen to lie side by side on the bed, without getting wet.

In the midst of all this, Ferdia caught Cú Chulainn off guard with a lunge of his great sword, burying it deep in the Ulsterman's side. Cú Chulainn groaned mightily, as his blood reddened the waters around him, and he called at last to Laeg, to pass him the *gae bolga*. When Ferdia heard the mention of this dread name, he moved his shield instantly, protecting the lower part of his body. But, it was too late. Cú Chulainn had already sent the fatal spear skimming over the water's surface. It pierced Ferdia's armour and passed right through his torso, so that its bloodied point could be seen on the other side.

'Enough,' cried Ferdia, 'I die by that.' And Cú Chulainn rushed towards him, lifted him up in his arms and carried him to the Ulster side of the ford. There, he made loud and lengthy lamentations over his fallen companion, before instructing Laeg to strip the body and remove the *gae bolga*.

'Before this fight, every combat was nothing more than a game, a piece of sport,' he told his faithful charioteer. 'Every combat was meaningless until Ferdia came to the ford. This thing will prey on my mind forever. For, yesterday, he was mightier than a mountain and today there is naught left of him but shadows.'

THE AWAKENING OF ULSTER

The battle with Ferdia sapped every last reserve of Cú Chulainn's strength. Once the remains of his childhood friend had been attended to, he collapsed by the ford and was borne away to his camp. There the healers nursed his wounds, for there was scarcely an inch of his body that had not suffered some gash or injury. Many grasses and charms were placed upon these sores but, even so, it was clear that he could no longer fight. 'Alas, Ulster,' moaned Cú Chulainn, 'who will defend you now?'

The answer lay in the stronghold at Emain Macha. There, Conchobar and the Ulstermen were recovering from their weakness. When they heard of Cú Chulainn's plight, they were immediately stirred into action. Conchobar set out that very day with thrice fifty of his chariots, bidding his fellow countrymen to come and join him.

Not far away, there was one in the Connacht camp who sensed this movement. Dubhthach the Black-Tongued dreamed of a great turmoil in the heavens. The sky turned a garish red, reflecting the carnage of a dreadful battle on the earth below. Everywhere, in his vision, he saw the spectacle of broken necks, mangled bodies and rivers of blood draining away into Ireland's soil.

And, while Dubhthach's sleeping form shook with the horror of this vivid dream, Nemain the Venomous came and spread her panic throughout the Connacht camp. A hundred warriors awoke from their slumber in a fearful sweat and died of fright. Ailill was greatly concerned when he learned of these omens. At once, he despatched the herald Mac Roth to scour the countryside, to see if there was any cause for alarm.

Obediently, Mac Roth went off to survey the plain from the vantage point at Slieve Fuad. He had not long to wait before he heard a sound so loud that he thought the heavens were falling in; then he noticed that the land was swarming with wild beasts, which had suddenly appeared from the depths of the nearby woods. Finally, he saw a heavy mist, filling the glens and the valleys, and in the mist sudden sparks and flashes of many colours could be seen.

'What do you think this means?' Ailill asked Fergus, when he heard the report.

'That is simple,' Fergus replied. 'This is the warrior men of Ulster, recovered from their weakness. It is they who have come into the wood. The vastness of their forces and the sound of their marching have terrified the beasts that live there, forcing them out onto the plain. As for the mist, that is the breath of the Ulstermen, as they head towards us. The lights and flashes are the glints of sunlight on their armour, and the fierce eyes of warriors intent on battle.'

'Is that all?' said Ailill. 'Then, let them come. We have men enough to deal with them.'

'You will need them,' warned Fergus, 'for nowhere in Ireland or the western lands; from

Greece and Scythia to the Orkneys or the Pillars of Hercules; from the Tower of Bregon to the island of Gades; in none of these places is there a force that can equal the Ulstermen in their full rage and glory.'

THE FINAL BATTLE

When, at last, the two great armies moved forward to meet each other, Cú Chulainn was still lying on his bed, sorely stricken with his wounds. From the sounds on the plain, however, he could tell that the army of the Ulstermen was drawing near and that battle would soon commence. He could also hear the croaking voice of the Morrigán, as she taunted the warriors of both sides, boasting that she would soon be picking the dead flesh from their bones. Cú Chulainn wanted to rise up and join the fray. But his underlings feared that his wounds would open up again, so they tied ropes and fastenings about him, to make sure that he could not move.

Then Cú Chulainn called out to his charioteer, to watch the progress of the battle and report to him all that occurred. And Laeg described how a little herd of cattle had broken away from Ailill's camp, and how the servants of both sides had rushed to try and take control of it.

'That little herd on the plain is the harbinger of a great battle,' said Cú Chulainn, knowingly, 'for that will certainly be the famed Brown Bull of Cooley with his heifers, the cause of all this strife and anguish.'

Then, as the sun rose higher in the sky, Laeg went out again, to see how the battle was faring.

Now, the two armies had clashed in earnest and were engaged in bitter hand-to-hand combat. Throughout the morning hours, neither side gained any real advantage. So, while Medb's warriors might make a breach in one part of the Ulster defences, this was soon matched by a surge from Conchobar's men in another part. Cú Chulainn lamented greatly on hearing this, swearing that his presence would have made all the difference.

When Medb saw that the battle was reaching a stalemate, she turned to Fergus, saying, 'It is time you went out to challenge Conchobar, to repay us for the hospitality you have enjoyed in Connacht.'

Then Fergus took up his sword and cut a swathe through the ranks of Ulster, killing a hundred men in his first attack. Medb and Ailill followed in his wake and, between them, they forced the Ulstermen to retreat three times.

Conchobar was alarmed at this turn of events, and he went to see what was driving his people back. Soon, he found himself in front of Fergus. Swiftly, he raised up his shield, Ochain the Screamer. Lavish to behold, with its four gold horns and its four gold coverings, the Ochain was an enchanted shield that cried out when its master was in danger. Three times Fergus brought his blade down upon it with full force, but the shield was not even dented. Instead, it screamed aloud, and all the shields of Ulster screamed along with it.

'Who holds this shield?' asked Fergus.

'A better man than you,' was Conchobar's reply. 'I am the one who drove you into exile.'

Then Fergus knew that it was Conchobar before him and his fury was raised to a greater pitch. He lifted his sword, the mighty Cladcholg, and was about to strike, when Cormac rushed forward and threw himself at Fergus's feet. On his knees, he pleaded with the Ulsterman not to betray his native land by striking down its king. Fergus paused for a moment and then agreed, provided that Conchobar retreated from the head of his forces. Then, instead of severing the king's head, he turned his sword aside and sliced off the tops of three small hills.

Cú Chulainn, meanwhile, had heard the sound of Ochain's screams and called out to Laeg:

'Tell me, who has dared to strike three blows against the king?'

'It is Fergus, that most valiant of warriors, and now his sword is laying low the men of Ulster.'

On hearing this, Cú Chulainn mustered all his remaining strength. He threw off the ropes and scattered the healing grasses in the air. Then he called for his weapons and for his twenty-seven tunics to be placed about him. As these were being tied, the fury came upon him, opening up all his wounds. But, in his frenzied state, Cú Chulainn felt neither pain nor weakness. Indeed, such was his impatience that he did not wait for his chariot to be harnessed. Instead, he lifted the carriage onto his back and headed down towards the battle.

Once in the fray, he used the chariot as a massive club, smiting all who came before him. Before long, he came face to face with Fergus. Now, his anger cooled and he spoke with the mild words of a foster-son: 'Go back, Fergus. Remember your promise to me.'

'Who is it that calls to me thus, in the heat of battle?' asked Fergus.

'It is I, Cú Chulainn. Remember how you came to me at the ford, Fergus. You had no sword in your scabbard and yet you asked me to yield to you. In return, you promised to yield to me on another occasion. That time has come. Yield to me now, Fergus. Remember your promise.'

'I remember it,' he said.

With these words, Fergus turned away and left the battlefield, taking with him his troop of three thousand men. And all the men of Ireland turned, when they saw this, and took to their heels.

Cú Chulainn and the Ulstermen pursued them, slaughtering them as they fled. It had been midday when the Hound of Culann arrived on the scene, and the sun was just beginning to set when the last of his foes made their escape over the ford.

Fergus watched from a distance, as Medb's army was scattered to the winds.

'This comes from following the lead of a woman,' he muttered to himself. 'A mare will always lead a herd astray.'

After the cattle raid of Cooley, Medb and Ailill made their peace with Conchobar. The Ulstermen went back to Emain Macha in triumph and, for the next seven years, there was friendship between Connacht and Ulster.

But Medb had not forgiven the Hound of Culann for thwarting her ambitions. During the years of peace, she sought out others who had a grievance against him: widows whose husbands had perished at the ford; children who had lost a father or a brother during one of his onslaughts. Then she set about schooling them for revenge.

At last, on the appointed day, Medb sent the three one-eyed daughters of Calatin to weave their spells on Cú Chulainn, robbing him of his strength. While he was weakened, his enemies came against him and slew him by a pillar stone. The bloodied head was carried back to Emer, who cleansed it of all wounds and wrapped it in a silken cloth. As she wept she heard a voice chiding her tears and bidding her remember her husband's glories. Looking up, she saw a vision of Cú Chulainn, riding in his chariot and singing the sweet music of the Sidhe.

The Fionn Cycle

THIS IS IRELAND'S EQUIVALENT to the Arthurian cycle. Finn is the noble champion, who leads a band of warriors known as the Fianna. He has no Excalibur, though he owns a Tooth of Knowledge, which helps him to guide his followers through a series of perilous adventures. When they are not fighting, the men of the Fianna enjoy a life of ease, engaging in endless bouts of hunting and feasting. The magic of the fairy people still poses a threat, but their time, like that of the Fianna itself, is drawing to a close. The chime of the Christian bell sounds a death knell for the age of heroes.

The Boyhood of Finn

In the days when Conn of the Hundred Battles claimed kingship over all Ireland, a bloody dispute arose between the sons of Baiscne and the sons of Morna. At the heart of this quarrel, there was a woman: Muirne of the White Neck, the beautiful daughter of a druid named Tadg.

Many men came to woo the maiden, but Tadg turned them all away. The most persistent of these suitors was Cumhal, the head of the Baiscne clan and leader of the Fianna, a warrior-band under Conn's command. He, too, was rejected, but this proved no deterrent, for he was convinced that Muirne loved him. So, under cover of darkness, he came to her chamber and carried her off by force. Immediately, Tadg went to Conn to complain about the actions of his officer.

Now Conn sent out messengers to Cumhal, ordering him to restore the girl to her father. Defiantly, however, Cumhal refused to yield her up.

'Everything I own,' he declared, 'I would willingly hand over to my lord, but the woman that I love remains with me.'

Conn was enraged by these defiant words and he despatched a force to seize back the woman. This force was headed by Aedh, the leader of the people of Morna.

The two armies met at Cnucha, where a bitter battle was fought. Many men became food for the crows before that day was spent. Eventually, though, Cumhal was slain and his treasure bag was carried off by Lia of Luachar, one of the followers of Aedh. Nor did the latter escape unharmed. A spear put out one of his eyes and, from that day forth, he was always known as Goll, which means 'the one-eyed man'.

And, because of these hurts, there was enmity from that time on between the sons of Morna and the sons of Baiscne.

After the battle, Muirne found that she was pregnant. In due course, she gave birth to a son, whom she named Demna. The child was fair and sturdy of limb, but Muirne dared not keep him, for she feared the wrath of the people of Morna. So, the boy was spirited away by two of her women, Bodball the Druidess and Liath Luachra. They took Demna to a cabin in the forest of Slieve Bladhma, where they reared him in secret.

He grew up straight and strong and fair-haired. Then, all too soon, the women told him that it was time to leave the forest, for they had learned that the sons of Morna were hunting for him nearby. So Demna bade them farewell and embarked on his travels. His first stop was near the stronghold of Mag Lifé. There, he saw a group of youths playing at hurley and went over to join them. They put one quarter of their number against him, but Demna still triumphed, winning game after game with ease. Immediately, the defeated lads went to their lord and told him of these remarkable feats.

'Who is this youth?' asked the chieftain warily. 'Describe him to me.'

'He told us his name was Demna,' they replied. 'As to his looks, they are handsome indeed, for his locks are long and fair.'

'Then his name should be Finn,' declared the lord and all were agreed, since this was the Irish word for 'fair'. 'Challenge him again tomorrow,' he continued, 'for I would not have it thought that our youths can be bested by a stranger.'

The young men of Mag Lifé did as they were commanded. Next morning they approached Demna, hailing him by his new nickname, and challenged him to wrestle with them in the lake. He agreed willingly and joined them in the water. Many youths came against Demna, but he threw them all off, drowning nine of them in the process.

News of this was carried back to the stronghold. 'Who has performed such a deed?' was the cry.

'It was Finn,' answered the survivors and, from that day on, he was always called by his nickname.

After this, Finn's travels took him on to Lough Leane, where he entered the service of the ruler of Bantry. He mentioned nothing of his parentage but, upon seeing the lad's skill at hunting, the king remarked: 'If I did not know otherwise, I would swear that you were the son of Cumhal for, in all my days, I never saw a better huntsman than he.'

This comment worried Finn and, fearing that the truth about his identity might be guessed, he decided to move on.

Next, he came to Carraighe, a land in the far west, where he joined the royal household. Here too, Finn's sojourn was all too short. One day, he was playing chess with his master and won seven games in a row. Now the king was proud of his skill at this game, and he looked closely at the youth.

'Who are you?' he enquired.

'I am the son of a peasant, my lord; one of the Luagne people from Tara,' Finn replied.

The king frowned. 'You are no peasant,' he growled. 'You are Muirne's son, the one whom the sons of Morna are seeking. Quit this place today. I do not want you killed, whilst you are under my protection.'

So, once again, Finn was obliged to continue his wanderings. This time he travelled north to Connacht, hoping to find Crimall, the son of Trenmor, who had been well acquainted with his father. On the way, however, he was distracted by the sound of a woman's voice, weeping and wailing. Immediately, Finn left the path, hastening to see what was amiss. It was not long before he found the woman in question, sitting disconsolately at the edge of a forest, with blood streaming down her face. 'What has happened here?' he enquired.

'We have been attacked,' replied the woman tearfully. 'A warrior came and killed my only son, Glonda, leaving me as you see me now.'

She feebly raised her arm, pointing out to Finn the direction that the villain had taken.

Finn followed swiftly in pursuit, tracking the man like a wild beast. Soon, the fellow came into view. Hearing footsteps behind him, he turned round and pulled out his sword. He was much larger than the fair-haired youth, but this did not deter Finn. Hurling himself forward, he laid into the man with his blade. For a few brief moments, the sound of clashing swords echoed through the forest, before a lusty blow from Finn's blade split open his opponent's skull.

Before departing, the lad went over to the dead man's horse, to see if it carried any clue to his identity. Much to his delight, he discovered that his adversary had been Lia of Luachar, one of the men who had fought against his father at the battle of Cnucha. Better still, he had Cumhal's treasure bag with him. With keen anticipation, Finn picked it up, longing to see the fabulous objects which he knew it would contain. For Cumhal's sack was no ordinary container. It had magic in its very fibres and was renowned throughout all of Ireland as the Treasure Bag of the Fianna.

Among its marvels were the shirt and knife of Manannán Mac Lir, the sea-god; the belt and hook of Goibhniu, the smith-god; the silver shears of the king of Alban; and the horned helmet of the king of Lochlann. Besides all these, there were the bones of seven pigs, which had once belonged to King Easal of the Golden Pillars. The sons of Tuireann had brought these back to Ireland and, though to the casual observer they might have seemed dry and useless, these bones could supply any man with an endless supply of broth. And each of these treasures would only be present in the bag when the sea was at full tide; when the waters ebbed away, it would be empty.

The greatest marvel of all, however, was the bag itself, which was made out of crane-skin. No other material was ever smoother and more delicate than this, for it had once been the flesh of a living woman. Aoife was her name and she had been the lover of Ilbrec, son of Manannán, until jealousy drove them apart. Then, by a cruel enchantment, she was changed into a crane. For the rest of her life, Aoife remained in this form, always flying behind the shadow of her lover. Then, when death came to her, Manannán took pity on her and made her into a sack for his most prized possessions. From him, the bag was passed on to Lugh, who in turn handed it down to Cumhal.

Finn was overjoyed at his good fortune in retrieving this wondrous object, and he took it with him to show Crimall. The latter was now an old man, living in poverty in a desolate part of Connacht. There, he was surrounded by several former members of the Fianna, who kept him from starvation by doing his hunting for him. Crimall was delighted to see the son of his old friend, all the more so when the lad brought out Cumhal's treasure bag. With gladness in his heart, he agreed to look after this for the young man, for it was plain to him that, at some stage in the future, Finn would become a worthy leader of the Fianna.

In the meantime, the youth had other things on his mind. He had learned to hunt, he had learned to fight and now, he believed, it was time to learn the art of poetry. For in Ireland, poets were treated with veneration and were given protection by all men of honour. If he devoted himself to this calling, Finn reasoned, he might at last be safe from the vengeance of the sons of Morna.

So he travelled to the home of Finnegas or Finn Eces, the druid who lived by the banks of the River Boyne. Finnegas had lived in this place for seven years, hoping to catch sight of the Salmon of Knowledge. For it had been prophesied that whoever ate the salmon in its entirety would be blessed with boundless wisdom. This same prophecy also stated that the salmon would be eaten by one named Finn, and Finnegas had supposed that this referred to him. He had no suspicions, therefore, when a lad introducing himself as Demna asked to become his pupil. He willingly took the boy into his household and, in the months that followed, taught him all that he knew of the art of rhyme-making.

Then, one day, the druid witnessed a sight that brought him great joy. There, by the river's edge, lay the fish he had been waiting for. It was much larger than a normal salmon and, on its shiny skin, all the colours of the rainbow seemed to dance. Taking it up, Finnegas carried the salmon back to his house and told his pupil to cook it. However, he was careful to stress that the fish was for him alone and that on no account was the boy to taste it.

Finn did as he was told and, a little while later, the smell of cooked salmon wafted through the house. Finnegas sat at the table and, as the fish was brought to him, he asked the lad whether he had sampled any of it.

'No,' Finn replied, but there was hesitation in his voice, so the druid made him tell all. 'I have not eaten any part of it,' he continued, 'but, as I was cooking the fish, I burnt my thumb on it and sucked it to ease the pain.'

The druid was perplexed. 'You say your name is Demna and yet, according to the prophecy, it must be Finn. For, now that you have tasted it, only you can eat the salmon in its entirety.'

Finn then explained about his nickname and Finnegas understood all. He bade the lad sit down and take his fill of the salmon. By this means, he came to have the power of divination that was contained within the flesh of the Salmon of Knowledge. After this, whenever he wanted to know the future, all Finn had to do was chant the sacred poem, the *teinm laida*, and place a finger inside his mouth, on the Tooth of Knowledge.

Armed with this wondrous ability, Finn now felt confident enough to claim his inheritance. After bidding farewell to Finnegas, he set off on the road to Tara. He arrived there during the festival of Samhain, a season of peace in Ireland, when all disputes and quarrels are put aside. Because of this, Finn was greeted warmly by Conn and no mention was made of his father's transgressions. Indeed, the king gave him a favoured place at his feasting table, close to the royal throne.

Soon, the hall was filled with the aroma of cooked pork and the sounds of drunken mirth. Despite the lavishness of the banquet, however, Finn sensed an air of apprehension in his hosts. It was not long before the reason behind this became apparent.

When the men of Tara had finished feasting, Conn rose to his feet and addressed his people: 'My friends, the eve of Samhain draws near once more. At that dread moment, the goblin Aillen will come amongst us and lull us all to sleep with his sweet fairy music. Then, while we slumber, he will blow fireballs from his disgusting jaws and set light to our beloved Tara. Each year he reduces our glorious palace to ashes, and each year we must rebuild it again from nothing. Is there none amongst you who can save us from this fate? Great would be the reward for such a man.'

Finn saw his chance. Rising from his seat, he called out to Conn: 'I can help you, my lord, if you will only grant me my father's inheritance. Will you make me the head of the Fianna, if I can defeat this terrible creature?'

'Certainly,' replied Conn and, in front of all his druids, he made a solemn oath to grant Finn's wish, if he could protect Tara from the flames.

Now there was amongst the company a man named Fiacha Mac Conga. He had been a close friend of Finn's father and was anxious to help the lad. In private, he came to him and offered to lend him an enchanted spear that was in his possession. He showed him how to use its magic properties, but warned the youngster that Aillen was a dangerous foe and would surely kill him if he failed.

The days went by and Samhain time came round. The dead rose from their tombs and spirits from the Otherworld were released into the realms of man. Then, as darkness fell, the goblin Aillen crept through the misty plain and arrived at Tara itself. Once there, he began to play his song of enchantment. Its strains were so soft and plaintive that wounded men forgot their hurts and women in labour were soothed into a honeyed sleep.

Immediately, Finn followed the instructions that Fiacha had given him. He stripped the magic spear of its coverings and placed its sharpened point firmly against his forehead. The touch of the naked metal filled him with superhuman strength.

High Kings

MANY OF THE MOST colourful tales of ancient Ireland are set in a period in which the dividing line between history and myth is very blurred. Nowhere is this more evident than in the vexed question of kingship. It will soon be obvious to the reader that the stories feature a bewildering plethora of kings, and it is often difficult to assess the precise hierachy.

The Petrie Crown
This decorated bronze head-dress may have been worn on ritual occasions. Another cone would have been attached to give the impression of horns.

Essentially, there were three types of king in early Ireland: petty kings, provincial kings and the high king. The petty kings ruled over small clusters of agricultural communities and were effectively tribal chieftains. They owed allegiance to the kings of the province or *cóiced*. The numbers of provinces varied somewhat but, for most of the mythological period, there were five (the literal meaning of *cóiced* is 'fifth'). These were Munster, Leinster, Connacht, Ulster, and the middle kingdom of Meath. The provincial rulers, in turn, obeyed the high king, who was always based at Tara.

The nature and role of the high king changed considerably over the course of time. Initially, though, his primary function was almost certainly a ritual one. For it was long believed that the ruler's fortune and character were intimately bound up with the prosperity of his land. Accordingly, the prospective king took part in a ritual marriage to the earth, thereby, it was hoped, ensuring the fertility of the country's crops and herds.

In the myths, this mystic union was sometimes represented as an encounter between the king and a goddess, personifying the land. One such story concerned Niall of the Nine Hostages, the ancestor of the Uí Néill dynasty. On a particular day, when he was out riding with his companions, he came across a hideous old crone. She brought them to a halt and demanded that one of the party give her a kiss. All refused, apart from Niall. Then, as their lips met, the hag turned into a beautiful woman called Flaithius ('Royalty'), who informed him that he would become the greatest of the high kings.

CHOOSING A KING

The legends also give some indication of the symbolic ceremonies that might have taken place at Tara. Divination seems to have played an important part. In *The Destruction of Da Derga's Hostel*, for example, Conaire Mór was chosen as high king after a ritual 'bull feast', organized by the druids. This prophesied that the next king would be found at daybreak, walking naked along the road to Tara with a stone in his sling. Conaire duly met these conditions.

The high kings were also required to pass certain other tests. They had to touch a sacred stone, the Lia Fáil, which would emit a piercing cry if the correct candidate had been chosen. Equally, they had to be the right size for both the royal chariot and cloak. Most important of all, they had to be in perfect physical condition. This proved a problem for Nuada, one of Finn's ancestors. He was made king of the Tuatha Dé Danaan and led them to a notable victory against the Firbolg. In the process, however, he lost one of his hands. Dian Cécht, the finest of his healers, managed to fashion him a new one out of silver. Even so, Nuada was forced to abdicate, for it was decreed that no man with a blemish could rule as king in Ireland.

According to ancient bardic listings, there were 188 high kings, beginning with Slaigne the

The Lia Fáil Stone *This stone is part of the mystical landscape at Tara, seat of the high kings. It may be the stone that was used in the ancient ceremony to choose a new king.*

Firbolg and continuing through to the twelfth century. For most of this time, however, the extent of the high king's power is questionable. Often, it did not seem to involve much more than possession of Tara itself. Many of the earliest rulers, however colourful their portrayal in the legends, have little historical substance. This is true even of the noble Cormac Mac Art, who may have ruled from AD 254–277 and who cut such a glorious figure in the Fionn cycle, where he was hailed as the patron of the Fianna.

The historical background becomes clearer with the emergence of the Uí Néill dynasty in the sixth century but, by this time, the spread of Christianity had begun to undermine the importance of Tara. After this, the most powerful of the high kings was Brian Boru, who managed to rally much of the country behind him, before his death at the Battle of Clontarf in 1014.

This enabled Finn to remain awake, even as Conn's fiercest guards were lulled into a heavy slumber. At length, when Aillen thought that all was safe, he stepped out of the shadows and opened wide his jaws. From these, there came a roaring flame, hot enough to turn the court of Tara into cinders. Swiftly, Finn leapt forward to face him. He raised his cloak to meet the flame and all of Aillen's heat was spent on it.

When the goblin saw that his magic had failed him, he turned and ran. Like a demon, he sped to his fairy dwelling at Slieve Fuad, thinking that no one would dare to follow. But Finn pursued him and, when he came within reach, he hurled Fiacha's magic spear. His aim was true and Aillen's slithery frame was nailed to the nearest tree. Now Finn beheaded him and placed his ugly skull upon a pole. This he brought back in triumph to Tara, where Conn and his people did him honour. With one accord, they made him leader of the Fianna, a duty which Finn fulfilled until the end of his days.

The Hounds of Tuiren

It happened once that Muirne came to visit Finn at the palace of Almu, accompanied by her daughter, Finn's half-sister, Tuiren. During their stay, the latter fell in love with Ullan Eachtach, one of the leading men of the Fianna. He asked for her hand in marriage and Finn consented, providing that he would promise to return the maid, if she should become unhappy. Ullan agreed willingly and the wedding went ahead without delay. A few months later, Tuiren announced that she was with child. Finn and his people were overjoyed.

It was not long, however, before the happiness of the newly-weds was threatened. For, prior to his marriage, Ullan had given certain promises to a woman of the Sidhe, Uchtdealb of the Fair Breast. She was consumed with jealousy and resentment against his bride and, putting on the guise of a messenger, she went to seek out Tuiren.

'Greetings, fair lady,' she began. 'I am sent by Finn to bring you to his feasting table, for he is anxious to celebrate his sister's good fortune.'

'I will happily accept this honour,' said Tuiren, 'but I should wait for my husband, for Finn would wish him to accompany me.'

'He is already at the palace, eager to see you,' continued Uchtdealb. 'Come, lady, we should go there without delay.'

Suspecting nothing, Tuiren did as she was told. But, as soon as they were out of the house, Uchtdealb brought out her dark druid rod and struck her victim across the face. Tuiren shrank back, screaming, as her human form fell away. A moment later, she found herself transformed into the shape of a hound.

Without delay, Uchtdealb put a leash on the unfortunate woman and led her to the house of Fergus Fionnliath. There, she handed over the dog, telling Fergus that Finn had charged him to look after it. The reason, she explained, was that the animal was with young and, therefore, could not be taken out hunting with the other dogs. Now it was well known among the Irishmen that Fergus hated dogs above all other creatures, and would never allow one to cross his threshold. Of course, he dared not oppose the will of his master and so agreed to take the dog in. By this means, however, Uchtdealb hoped to be revenged upon her rival, believing that she would spend the rest of her days in a household where she was hated and reviled.

But the fairy woman had reckoned without the sweetness of Tuiren's nature. She was so gentle and affectionate, always licking the hand of her keeper, that his harshness quickly melted away. Within a short space of time, the hound was given pride of place in the house, eating by Fergus's table and sleeping by the warmth of his hearth. After some months had passed, she gave birth to two fine whelps, which Fergus nurtured fondly, for he had now developed a huge liking for hounds of every kind.

In the meantime, Tuiren's absence was causing concern. Finn, who had been looking forward to the birth of his sister's children, was greatly angered when he heard that she was no longer living with Ullan. Immediately, he ordered the warrior to fulfil his marriage pledge and return Tuiren to him. This command filled Ullan with dread, for he was terrified of the punishments that Finn would inflict upon him, when he realized that his sister had gone missing.

In desperation, Ullan went to seek Uchtdealb, hoping that she might use her fairy powers to help him find his wife. But the woman of the Sidhe looked grimly at him. 'Why have you come to me with your troubles?' she enquired. 'Have you forgotten the false promises which you made me?'

Ullan hung his head in shame. 'I confess, my lady, that I have treated you most ill. Now do I regret my actions with all my heart. Even so, help me, I implore you. Otherwise, my life will be forfeited to Finn, for having lost his sister.'

Uchtdealb considered this slowly. 'I may help you,' she said at last, 'for I know where I can find your wife. But there is a condition. If I protect you from the wrath of Finn, you must give up Tuiren and remain with me till the end of your days. Choose now, Ullan, for I will give you no other chance to save yourself.'

The warrior did not hesitate. At once, he accepted Uchtdealb's offer and promised that she would have his heart forever. This delighted the fairy woman and she kept her part of the bargain. Without delay, she travelled to the house of Fergus Fionnliath and brought away Tuiren and the two whelps. Then she gave back the woman her true shape and handed her over to Finn. About the dogs, however, she could do nothing, for she had placed no enchantment upon them. Nevertheless, Finn took them into his household, naming them

Bran and Sceolan. And, from that time forth, he cherished them dearly, treating them with all the favour he would have shown to his royal nephews.

THE BIRTH OF OISIN

One day, not long after this, Finn and his faithful companions went out hunting in the countryside around Almu. They had not gone far, when a beautiful fawn rushed across their path. Immediately, the entire party set out after it, each man eager to be the one to capture such a prize. But the fawn was fleet of foot and it outran the huntsmen with ease. One by one, the pursuers gave up the chase, until only Finn and his two hounds remained on its trail. They tore after the creature, but its stamina was as great as its speed, and it seemed certain that it would escape.

Then, just as Finn was about to admit defeat, the fawn stopped and sat down. Bran and Sceolan reached it first, but they did not harm it. Instead, they scampered round the fawn, licking its face and neck. Then, as the hounds ran back to Finn, the creature began to follow them. Indeed, it followed them all the way back to Almu. There, Finn gave orders that no one was to harm the beast and that it should be allowed to roam freely within the palace enclosure.

That same night, Finn woke suddenly from his sleep. Out of the shadows, he saw a woman coming towards him, her long hair shining in the candle-light. 'Do not be afraid,' she said softly, 'for I am no dream. My name is Sadb and I am the creature that you hunted today, returned to my human shape. Three years ago, Fear Doirche, the Dark Druid of the men of Dea, put me into this form for refusing his love. Ever since then, I have sought shelter in the woods and valleys of your land, always fearing that I might meet my end at the jaws of some huntsman's dog. Even today, I could not cease my flight until I had shaken off all but your two hounds, for I sensed that their nature was close to my own and that they would not kill me. Now, at last, I am free, for the druid's powers cannot reach within the walls of your palace.'

Finn was delighted by these tidings and invited the lady to stay with him. Shortly afterwards, they were married and great were the celebrations in Almu on that happy day. Then, for the space of a whole year, the couple were never parted. Out of love for her, Finn put aside all hunting and fighting, preferring to remain in Sadb's company.

Finally, at the end of the year, word reached his ears that invaders from Lochlann had landed on Ireland's shores. Reluctantly, Finn mustered his forces and prepared to leave. 'I must confront my enemies,' he explained to Sadb, 'for no man can truly live, if he allows his honour to die.'

She was saddened by his words, especially as she was now with child, but Finn promised that he would return as soon as possible.

For seven days, a fierce battle raged between the warriors of Lochlann and the heroes of the Fianna, before the foreigners fled back to their ships. Those seven days seemed like an eternity to Finn. Like a man possessed, he took the first opportunity to hurry homewards ahead of his army, so desperate was he to see his beloved wife once more. At last, the ramparts of Almu came into view and Finn strained his eyes, hoping for a precious glimpse of Sadb. To his surprise, there was no sign of her. Perhaps, he thought, she has not yet received word of my return. So he pressed his horse to go faster, expecting to find her inside the stronghold.

Upon his arrival, Finn rushed straight to Sadb's chamber, only to find it empty. Then, as he ran through the palace, he noticed an air of gloom about the place. Everyone avoided his gaze. 'Where is my wife?' he cried. 'Where is the flower of Almu? Why is she not here to meet me?'

Then one of Finn's people told him what had happened. 'After you left, my lord, Sadb would stand for hours upon the ramparts, watching out for your return. Then, two days ago, she gave a little shriek of delight and ran down to the great door. I looked out from my vantage point, wondering what had caused her to utter such a cry, and I saw a man in your likeness, waiting on the plain below. With him he had two hounds, which were identical in every way to Bran and Sceolan.'

'I thought it odd,' he continued, 'that you should wait outside the walls, rather than enter your home directly. But, as I have said, the man was your very twin …' At this point, the guard hesitated, as if about to make some excuse, until Finn motioned to him to carry on.

'Sadb ran towards the man with her arms outstretched and calling out her fondest greetings. But, no sooner did she touch this shadow of yourself, than she let out a terrible moan. For the stranger brought out a hazel wand from beneath his cloak and struck her with it. Within an instant, she was gone and, in her place, there stood the very fawn that followed you home a year ago. Three times the creature turned and tried to run back to Almu but, on each occasion, the dogs bared their teeth and took the fawn by the throat, dragging it back to their master. When we saw these things, we picked up our weapons and rushed out to help your lady. But it was too late. By the time we reached that spot, the man, the dogs and the fawn had all vanished, and no trace of them could be found.'

Now Finn was overcome with a deep sense of sorrow. In his heart, he knew that this stranger was Fear Doirche, the Dark Druid, who had come to reclaim the woman he had lost. Straight away, he went to his chamber, where he remained for a night and a day, refusing all food and uttering not a single word. Then he called for his horse and his favourite hounds, determined to try and track Sadb down. He had found her once, he reasoned, so it should be possible to pick up her trail a second time. But the hunt proved fruitless. Finn returned empty-handed that night, after hours of searching. He was tired, hungry and disappointed, but not dismayed. On the morrow, he resolved, he would try his luck again.

For seven long years, Finn scoured the countryside, riding alone through every dark forest and every remote glen. During this time, the only

hounds that he would take with him were Bran and Sceolan, for he feared that any other dog might do some harm to Sadb. Eventually, however, Finn was forced to admit that the cause was hopeless. At the end of the seven years, he gave up looking for Sadb and began hunting again with his companions, as he had done in the past.

Then, one day, while the Fianna were out on a chase near Ben Bulben, a strange thing happened. All of a sudden, they heard a fierce outcry from the hounds, as if they had cornered some savage quarry. Rushing to investigate, Finn and his companions came upon a naked young boy with long, flowing hair. The dogs were growling viciously at this child, as if it were some wild creature of the forest, but Bran and Sceolan were protecting it. Then, as soon as the Fianna had quietened down the pack, the two dogs went over to the boy and began to lick him affectionately.

Finn wondered at this marvel. Then, looking closely at the child, he fancied that he could see some likeness of Sadb in his features. Could this be the baby that she had been carrying at the time of her abduction? Swiftly, he gave orders that the lad should be brought back to Almu and raised in his household.

It was not long before the boy lost some of his wildness, growing up like other children. Then, little by little, as he learned the use of speech, he told them all he could remember about his early days. He had known no mother or father, he said, but only a kindly fawn, which cared for him most tenderly. They lived in a secluded valley, shut in on every side by towering cliffs, which prevented them from wandering far. In the summer, they fed on fresh fruit and roots while, in the winter, they relied on a store of food, left out for them in a cave. Finn's ears pricked up at this. Who, he wondered, was providing this food?

The answer came soon enough, for the boy went on to mention a tall, shadowy figure, who used to visit them frequently. Stern was his countenance; dark and forbidding were his moods. On some occasions, he would speak softly to the fawn while, on others, he would shout and rail at it,

uttering fearsome threats. Whatever his approach, the fawn's reaction would always be the same. Without exception, she would shrink back from him, filled with a mixture of loathing and disgust. After this, the man would leave them, cursing under his breath.

There came a day when the stranger's voice seemed to carry an added note of menace. As always, he spoke at length to the fawn, sometimes cajoling and sometimes threatening. This time, however, he did not give up. Instead, he brought out a hazel wand and struck them with it. The touch of this rod, the boy remembered, filled him with a strange sensation. When he looked up, he could see that the fawn was following the man, though only under the force of some compulsion, for her eyes were full of dread and sorrow.

He, for his part, tried to follow them, but his legs would not obey him. They were rooted to the spot and, no matter how hard he struggled, he could not move. About that moment, he could remember nothing more, save only the piteous sounds of the fawn and her sorrowful, backward glances as she was dragged away. After that, his senses began to swim and he fell into a deep sleep. When he awoke, he was on the side of a hill, on the very spot where Bran and Sceolan discovered him. And, though he hunted far and wide, he could never again find the valley where he had lived with the fawn.

Finn grieved deeply, when he heard this sad tale about the fawn and the Dark Druid. Then he claimed the boy as his son and gave him the name of Oisin, which means 'Little Fawn'. In time, he grew up to be a valiant warrior and one of the greatest chiefs of the Fianna. But of his mother, the fair Sadb, nothing more was ever heard. Though Finn looked forward to every hunt, nursing a secret hope that the same fawn might cross his path once more, he never saw his beloved again.

Celtic Festivals

T HE CELTIC YEAR featured four ceremonial festivals: Samhain, Imbolc, Beltane and Lughnasadh. These were held at three-monthly intervals, beginning with Samhain at the end of October. Initially, the festivals were designed to aid farming communities, by marking different stages in the agricultural or pastoral year. Their appearance in the legends, however, is usually linked with the rituals that occurred on these dates.

SAMHAIN

The most important festival was Samhain, which ushered in the new year. This was celebrated on the evening of 31 October and throughout the following day. As part of its rites, old fires were extinguished and then relit, amid great ceremony, from a sacred flame watched over by the druids. In farming terms, Samhain marked the period when cattle were brought in from the fields and slaughtered. More significantly, though, it was also a festival of the dead. According to Celtic belief, this meant that the souls of the departed could return to the world of the living and warm themselves in their former homes. Sinister spirits from the Otherworld were also released, often with dire consequences for the mortals who crossed their path.

The magical and supernatural overtones of Samhain were given great play in the legends.

Bronze head of St Brigid
St Brigid is the Christianized Irish goddess Brigantia. She was linked to the festival of Imbolc on 1 February, which celebrated fertility.

Aillen, the fire-breathing goblin who appears in *The Boyhood of Finn* at Samhain to burn down Tara, is typical of the malevolent creatures that were pitted against the Irish heroes. Equally, because of its close links with the supernatural, Samhain proved a particularly auspicious time for the casting of spells, and many of the shape-shifting episodes in the stories coincide with it. The festival also affected the attitudes of both men and gods. It was this, for example, which enabled Oenghus to trick the Dagda into giving him his home. Similarly, it gave Finn the opportunity to be reconciled with the king of Tara and put an end to the blood-feud which had threatened his early life.

The festival of Samhain was later Christianized as All Saints' or All Hallows' Day, but echoes of the darker aspects of the festival can be found in the mischief-making at Hallowe'en and in the many superstitions associated with the period. In Wales, for example, there was a belief that a wind, which blew over the feet of a corpse, would carry dreadful sighs to the houses of those who were due to die in the coming year. In a similar vein, one Irish superstition advised that anyone who heard footsteps behind them on Hallowe'en should take care not to look round. For, it was said, these were the footsteps of the dead and, if you gazed into their hollow eyes, you would surely die.

OTHER FESTIVALS

The remaining festivals figure less often in the early myths, though there are some compelling links with Ireland's past. Imbolc (1 February), for example, is closely associated with St Brigid, whose feast is celebrated on the same day. Apart from the fact that she established a religious community at Kildare, almost nothing is known about the real life of the saint. Instead, early accounts of her life were packed with supernatural details, which probably originated as anecdotes about a pagan goddess called Brigit, or Brigantia, a daughter of the Dagda. She was raised, it was said, in the household of a druid and was suckled with the milk of Otherworld cows. Then, as an adult, she possessed a larder with an ever-replenishing stock of food. Stories of this kind were used by the early Church authorities, to help smooth the transition from paganism to Christianity.

Beltane (1 May) was the most enduring of the Celtic festivals. Essentially, it was a fire festival, marked by the lighting of bonfires on hilltops and other sacred places at the beginning of the summer. In common with Samhain, however, its most lasting associations were with the supernatural. On the eve of Beltane, spirits and witches were said to roam abroad, a tradition which survived in the celebrations of Walpurgis Night. Lughnasadh (1 August) took its name from Lugh, the sun-god, who featured prominently in the early Irish epics. His influence was particularly strong in the Ulster cycle, where he was hailed as the father and protector of Cú Chulainn. The festival itself was linked to the gathering in of the harvest, a notion which survived in the Christian feast of Lammas ('loaf-mass'), which superseded it.

Fourknocks Stone *At Samhain and Beltane, the spirits of the Otherworld, believed to reside at sites such as Fourknocks, were released into the mortal world.*

The Curse of the Quicken Trees

Many were the perils which Finn and his warriors faced, during the glorious days of the Fianna. Many were the times when it seemed that Ireland's brave fighters might be swept away by evil foes. Amongst all of these, however, none proved more deadly than Midac and his palace of the quicken trees.

The seeds of the trouble were sown in the early days of the Fianna, shortly after Finn had assumed command. From across the Northern Sea, an invading force came from the distant kingdom of Lochlann, headed by its powerful leader, Colga of the Hard Weapons. His army ravaged the eastern provinces, bringing death and destruction in their wake. But Colga had reckoned without the wrath of the Fianna. When their armies met, they fought out a fierce and raging battle until, as evening drew near, the foreigners were scattered to the winds. Then Finn gave orders for Colga and all his chieftains to be put to the sword. One alone survived. This was Midac, Colga's youngest son, whom Finn spared on account of his tender years.

The youth was brought up in Finn's household, where he was treated with noble generosity. No foster-son could have been shown greater favour. He was given fine clothes and servants; he was taught the skills of warfare and hunting; and when he came of age, he was admitted to the ranks of the Fianna itself. In spite of all this, Midac remained sullen and distant, harbouring a bitter grudge against the men who had killed his father.

After a time, the other members of the Fianna grew suspicious of the youth, fearing that he intended to commit some mischief against them. So they urged Finn to send Midac away from the stronghold at Almu, to prevent him from learning too many of their secrets. Finn considered this request and deemed it wise. Without further ado, he summoned the youth before him.

'You have reached an age,' he said, 'when it is fitting that you should leave our household and make a home of your own. Choose, therefore, the two districts of Ireland that please you best and they shall be yours. What is more, I will give you men and cattle, so that your existence there may be as pleasant as it has been here.'

'You are most generous, my lord,' replied Midac, bowing politely before Finn, though the tone of his voice was icy cold.

Shortly after, Midac made his choice, selecting land at Kenri on the River Shannon as his new home. He had good reason for settling on this territory, for its location was full of strategic potential. Here, the river opened out like a great sea, offering sheltered harbours and secluded islands, where an invading force might easily land in secret. Midac was very content, as Finn's people laboured to build him a fine stronghold for, at long last, he could see a way of gaining his revenge.

For fourteen years, Midac lived quietly in his new home, growing wealthier and more powerful with each passing year. The Fianna were scarcely aware of this, however, for Midac took care to make himself an outsider, never going near Finn's palace and allowing no one to set foot on his land.

Then, one day, Finn and the Fianna went out hunting on the plains of Hy Conall Gavra. The chase was good and, as dusk began to fall, they pitched camp on the hill of Knockfierna, not far from the district of Kenri. The tired huntsmen were resting before preparing their food, when they noticed a stranger walking towards them. He wore a mantle of red satin, a helmet of polished silver, and a long sword in an enamelled sheath. As he drew nearer, he greeted Finn politely and informed him that he was a poet.

'That is hard to believe,' declared Finn, 'for you have the appearance of a fine and noble warrior.'

'Nevertheless,' the other replied, 'I am indeed a poet. I can prove it by giving you a riddle. Tell me, if you can, who is the bright-faced queen, who lies on a couch of crystal and wears a robe of green. Her children are many and thin, but you can see them all clearly, if you gaze through her skin. She moves at a slow and stately speed, yet her pace can outrun the fastest steed. Can you tell me, my lord, who this wondrous woman may be?'

'That is easy,' answered Finn, swelling up with pride. 'The queen that you mention is Boann, the spirit of the River Boyne. Her couch of crystal is the sandy river-bed and her green robe is the grassy plain of Breg, through which the waters travel. Her children are the legions of fish, which swim in the Boyne and which you can see through its watery skin. Am I right?'

'You are indeed,' said the stranger with a smile.

'My lord,' said Conan Mail, one of the chiefs of the Fianna, 'you have done well to unravel this puzzle but, in so doing, you have ignored a still greater one. For the man who stands before you now is none other than Midac, who grew up in your household. We did not recognize him at first, because no one has seen him for the past fourteen years. Not once has he invited us to share the meat at his table. So, the real puzzle is: why has he come to us now, this master of ingratitude?'

'That is easily answered,' said Midac, his smile growing ever broader. 'I spotted your band when you were out hunting and I have come to offer you my hospitality. At this very moment, I have a grand banquet prepared, ready for all of you to enjoy. It is at my palace of the quicken trees, not far from this hill. Come, I pray you, and let me return the many favours that you have shown to me.' With these words, he turned round and pointed out the palace in the distance.

Finn accepted the invitation, promising that he and his warriors would join Midac there shortly. This answer satisfied Midac and he departed. Then Finn consulted with his companions, for there were few among them who trusted the word of Colga's son. Cautiously, they decided that a group of the Fianna should remain behind on the hill, ready to lend assistance if Midac's invitation should prove to be a trap. Diarmaid, Ficna and Fatha Conan were among this group, which was led by Oisin.

Once this had been agreed, Finn and his group of warriors set off towards Midac's palace. As they approached it, they were amazed at both its size and splendour. Indeed, they were surprised that word of such a magnificent house had not spread throughout all of Ireland. The structure seemed all the more impressive, because it stood high upon a grassy mound, surrounded by a thick plantation of quicken trees. These were covered in clusters of scarlet berries, which glistened like drops of blood. No birds pecked at these. In fact, nothing at all was stirring in the vicinity. An air of stillness hung over the place like a shroud.

This mood prevailed, even when they reached the main door. No attendants rushed to make them welcome or tend to their horses. Even so, the smell of cooking lured them in. Then, once inside, Finn and his companions could scarcely believe their eyes. Never before had they seen such a feasting hall. A great fire burned in the hearth, but it gave out no smoke, only a sweet scented air which wafted round the room. On either side of the banqueting table, there were fine couches, all decked out with soft furs and rich coverlets. Behind them, the walls of the chamber gleamed and sparkled with many colours, as if jewels had been set between the boards.

Nobody came to greet them, so Finn and his companions sat down and waited. Presently, a door opened and Midac walked into the room. He said nothing, but simply stared at his guests, gazing at each of the Fianna in turn. Then, a moment later, he wheeled round and went out of the chamber, shutting the great door behind him.

The warriors whispered amongst themselves, baffled by their host's peculiar behaviour. At length, Finn spoke up. 'I find it very strange, my friends, that we have been left here so long without attendance, and without either food or drink. Perhaps there has been some mistake, and we were actually meant to go to Midac's other stronghold, the palace of the island. Even so, I wonder greatly that such a mistake could have been made.'

'I see something stranger than this,' uttered Mac Luga of the Red Hand. 'Have you not noticed how the smoke from the fire, which recently seemed so fragrant and sweet, is now giving off clouds of thick, black soot?'

'I see something stranger still,' added Glas Mac Encarda. 'For the walls of this chamber, which I had thought so smooth and brightly-coloured, now appear to be nothing more than rough planks, crudely fastened together with willow bands.'

'I see another strange thing,' said Dathkeen the Strong-Limbed. 'When we entered this room, there were seven great doors, each of them opened wide and with a fine prospect of the river. Yet, now that I look again, there is just a single narrow door, which is fastened tight.'

'I see something stranger than all of these,' cried Conan Mail. 'A moment ago, we were sitting on soft couches, covered in luxurious furs, but all of these have now gone. Instead, we are sitting on the bare earth, which is as cold and damp as a winter snowfall.'

With this, he tried to climb to his feet, only to find that he was rooted to the spot. Then Conan let out a cry of anguish, which was soon echoed by his companions, for all of them found that they were in the same predicament.

For a few minutes, the chamber was filled with silence, until Dathkeen came up with a suggestion. 'I pray you, lord Finn, since it is clear that we are in danger here, could you not place your thumb upon the Tooth of Knowledge? Perhaps it might give us some clue of how we may escape from this accursed place.'

Finn thought this a sound idea and touched the magic tooth. For the next few minutes, no one spoke. Then Finn let out a loud sigh. 'Alas, dear friends, I have no good news to report. Even as we sit here, Midac is gathering a force at his other stronghold, ready to destroy us. At the head of this army are three kings from the Island of Torrents, each of whom can fight with the fury of a dragon. It is they who have trapped us here, for the soil of this palace comes from their enchanted land. And nothing can free us from this spot, save the blood of those same kings, sprinkled on the earth. Soon, they will come here and despatch us, while we are unable to defend ourselves. In the meantime, all we can do is sit here and wait to die.'

Away from the palace, the mood of Oisin's men was just as pessimistic. 'I fear that some mischief has befallen our comrades,' said Diarmaid. 'Otherwise, Finn would have sent back a messenger, to let us know that they were safe.'

The others shared this view, so Diarmaid and Ficna rode off down the hill to investigate. As they approached the palace of the quicken trees, they noticed the horses of the Fianna outside, alone and unattended. Stealthily, they dismounted and crept closer. Then, hearing the voices of Finn and his companions inside, Diarmaid called out to them, asking if all was well.

Finn's reply was immediate. 'Come no nearer, brave warriors, for there are dangerous enchantments at work in this place. Midac has lured us into a trap and nothing can save us, apart from the blood of the three kings from the Island of Torrents.' Then he explained to them Midac's plot, which had been revealed through his Tooth of Knowledge.

Diarmaid was undismayed. 'Never give up hope, my lord, for we will do our best to free you. Ficna and I will return now to Oisin and inform him of your plight. Together, we will ride against

them and, small though our force is, it may be that we can overcome them.'

Finn agreed to this and wished them luck. As he heard the two brave warriors leave, however, his heart was heavy, for he was sure that he would never see them again.

Now the route back to Oisin's force led through a narrow ford. As they approached this, Diarmaid and Ficna saw four men riding towards them. These were Midac and the three kings from the Island of Torrents, coming to kill Finn and his companions in the palace of the quicken trees. Such was their confidence in the power of their spells that they travelled alone to commit these terrible deeds.

Immediately, Diarmaid took aim and hurled his spear at Midac, piercing him through the neck. 'Alas,' cried the son of Colga, 'I am mortally wounded.' Then he tumbled to the ground and died. Seeing this, the three kings dug their heels in their horses and rushed towards the Irishmen. But the two heroes stood their ground, facing the onslaught as firmly as rocks meeting the oncoming waves. The contest was long and hard, with each man receiving hurts from the swords of his enemies. Eventually, though, Diarmaid's battle-frenzy won the day and, one by one, the three dragon-like kings were slain.

Exhausted, the victors walked unsteadily to the edge of the ford and began to bathe their wounds in its cool water. Suddenly, Diarmaid remembered Finn's words about the spell, which had sapped their comrades of all their strength. Swiftly, he urged Ficna to help him behead the fallen kings, before their blood seeped away into the earth. Then, bearing the severed heads before them, the pair swiftly returned to the palace of the quicken trees. There, they grasped the gory objects by the hair and shook them fiercely, so that thick droplets of blood spilled onto the palace floor.

By this means, Finn and his companions were freed from their enchantment. And, once the death of the three kings from the Island of Torrents became known, the army of warriors under their command fled away, swearing never to return to Ireland's shores.

Oisin in Tir na nÓg

Early one morning, when the dew lay thick on the ground, Finn and his companions went out hunting near Lough Leane. Their hounds had just roused some deer from the thickets, when a strange sight brought the chase to a halt. It was a beautiful maiden, riding slowly towards them on an elegant, snow-white steed. She wore a robe of dark brown silk, flecked with crimson stars, and a slender, golden coronet. Golden, too, were the hooves of her horse and the bridle that she held in her hand.

As she drew near, Finn called out to her: 'Who are you, fair lady, and what brings you to this place?'

'My name is Niamh,' the maid replied, 'and I have travelled far to meet with you, my lords of the Fianna. For I am the daughter of the king of Tir na nÓg, a distant land beyond the Western Sea. As to my purpose, that is easily said. I have come to find Oisin, the son of Finn. Much have I heard of his bravery and fine deeds and, though many men have sought my hand, I wished to meet with him first.'

'You do me too much honour, lady,' murmured Oisin, ambling gently towards her.

Niamh eyed him approvingly. 'I see you are as fair as your reports,' she said. 'Come with me now and let me show you my home. It is the most delightful place. All is rich and fertile. Fruit grows on the trees all year round and the rivers run with wine. A hundred warriors will feast with you, while a hundred harpers play sweet music. Come, and let my father shower you with gifts: a shield that can never be pierced, a sword which never misses its mark, and a helmet that will guard you from all dangers. Come, and you may defy the passage of time, for no one ever grows old in our land. Beauty, strength and good health shall always be yours. Come, take my hand, for I would be your wife.'

There was honey and silk in Niamh's words. While she spoke, a dreamy stillness fell upon the company. Nothing moved or stirred. The hounds did not whine, the horses did not shake their tails, and the leaves did not rustle in the breeze. Whether compelled by some enchantment or by the force of her beauty, Oisin felt unable to refuse her. 'Gladly will I go with you, my lady,' he declared, 'for you are fairer to me than any other maiden in the world.'

On hearing this the Fianna were dismayed. 'Alas,' said Finn, 'it saddens me to hear you say such a thing, for your journey seems such an arduous one that I doubt you will return.'

Nevertheless, Oisin had made up his mind. He bade his companions farewell and, without further ado, climbed up behind Niamh, on her snow-white horse. It moved slowly at first, until it reached the sea. Then the golden hooves took flight, skimming across the surface of the waves as swiftly as any gusting wind. Oisin gazed in wonder, as the billowing surf sped away beneath him.

They passed many curious spectacles on their journey. Lofty towers and palaces that glittered like glass loomed up briefly, before vanishing back into the haze. Once, Oisin fancied that he beheld a hornless stag bounding over the waves, pursued by a white hound with blood-red ears. Another time, he witnessed a young maid on a bay horse, hurrying across the water with a golden apple in her hand.

St Patrick

THE EARLY IRISH LEGENDS were written down and preserved during the Christian era, so it is hardly surprising that some chroniclers attempted to fuse the two traditions, inventing stories where some of the ancient heroes survived long enough to meet up with St Patrick and his fellow missionaries.

The best-known example of this occurs in the tale of *Oisin in Tir na nÓg*, when the son of Finn returns to Ireland, after spending three hundred years in the land of eternal youth. In doing so, he is introduced to St Patrick and becomes a guest in his household. At the end of the original story, there is a lengthy debate between the two men, when St Patrick tries to convert the old warrior. In vain the holy man regales him with the joys of the faith for, at every turn, Oisin begins to reminisce about happier times with Finn and his companions.

The Colloquy of the Old Men is another tale in a similar vein, dating back to the twelfth century. In this, Oisin and Cailte are the last survivors of the Fianna, more than a century after the death of Finn. The pair separate, with Oisin retiring into a fairy mound to join his mother, while Cailte heads south towards Tara. On the way, he meets up with St Patrick and the two men travel onwards together. The saint asks Cailte if he knows of a well, for he wishes to baptize the people of Bregia and Meath. The old warrior obliges, before embarking on the first of many anecdotes about the exploits of the Fianna. These mythical tales form the backbone of the Colloquy, even though they often have a Christian gloss. In particular, Finn's prophecy about the coming of St Patrick is repeated many times in the course of the narrative.

The links with the holy father were not confined to the characters from the Fionn cycle. There is also a lengthy, eleventh-century poem entitled *Cú Chulainn's Ghostly Chariot*. In this, the Ulster hero returns from the grave to give St Patrick an account of his deeds in Lochlann. Once again, the purpose of the work was to provide a bridge between Ireland's mythical past and its Christian present.

LEGENDS OF ST PATRICK

Of course, St Patrick himself was the focus of many legends. The most famous of these told of his confrontation with Laoghaire, the high king.

Cross of St Patrick and St Columba, Kells
The east face of the cross depicts the Fall of Man, the Children in the Fiery Furnace amd Daniel in the Lions' Den.

Shrine of St Patrick's Bell
This bronze casket, adorned with gold filigree and crystals, was commissioned in c. 1100 by Donal O'Loughlin, an Irish king.

Laoghaire, however, refused and the fire of Christianity was lit in Ireland. Other legends relate how Patrick banished the snakes from the island – the snake being a conventional symbol of Satan – and how he used the three leaves and single stem of the shamrock to teach Laoghaire about the nature of the Trinity.

Most information about the historical St Patrick (c. 390–461?) is derived from his autobiography (the *Confessio*). From this, we learn that he was born in western Britain, at a place called Bannavem Taburniae. He came from a prosperous Romano-British background, and his father was both a civil official and a deacon. After the withdrawal of the Romans, however, this comfortable society came increasingly under threat, as Irish raiders plundered the vulnerable coastal areas of Britain. At the age of sixteen, Patrick became a victim of one of these raids and was carried off to Ireland as a slave.

For the next six years, he was put to work as a herdsman, and it was during this time that he began to take an interest in the Bible. After his escape, he returned to Britain and decided to enter the priesthood. His training appears to have taken place at Auxerre in Gaul, where he was a pupil of St Germanus.

Patrick returned to Ireland in c. 432, apparently as a successor to Palladius, the first Irish bishop appointed by the papacy. According to tradition, he began his ministry at Saul in County Down, before establishing his main base at Armagh in 444. In time, this was to claim primacy over all other Irish churches. Patrick encouraged the growth of monasticism and, towards the end of his life, he went into retreat for forty days at Croagh Patrick in County Mayo, which is now the centre of an important pilgrimage. The saint left behind some writings, including a hymn called the Lorica (the Breastplate). Patrick's handbell and one of his teeth are said to be preserved in two shrines, now housed in Dublin's National Museum.

This took place on Easter Saturday in 432, a date which coincided precisely with a major pagan festival. As part of the rites, the druids were due to light a sacred flame on the hill of Tara and no other fires were to be lit before it. Patrick, however, was defiant. On the hill of Slane, which is visible from Tara, he lit his own flame. The druids were outraged and explained to Laoghaire that it should be extinguished immediately, or else it would burn forever.

Not far behind her, a noble youth with flowing yellow locks gave chase. Eagerness was in his eyes, though whether this was for the maid or the apple, no one could say. Oisin tried to quiz Niamh about these marvels, but she brushed his questions aside.

'Think nothing of these, my love. They are but trifles compared with the wonders that you will see in the land of Tir na nÓg.'

At last, they arrived at their destination. The sea mists parted and Oisin beheld a fertile plain, set with crystal lakes and distant blue hills. Nearer to the shore, there lay a splendid city, at the heart of which was a magnificent palace, encrusted with radiant gems and flakes of gold. Proudly, Niamh indicated to her betrothed that this was her home.

While Oisin marvelled at this spectacle, a troop of noble warriors came out of the palace to greet them. Thrice fifty champions were in this band, all kitted out in shining armour. At the head of this glittering host rode the king and queen of Tir na nÓg, impatient to see the man that their daughter had chosen as her husband. They greeted Niamh and Oisin warmly and led them back to the palace, where a sumptuous banquet had been prepared. For a full ten days, the feasting hall echoed with the sounds of loud rejoicing until, at last, Niamh of the Golden Hair became Oisin's bride.

The Irishman had no cause to regret his decision. Over the months that followed, life in Tir na nÓg proved every bit as pleasant as Niamh had predicted. The king and queen grew fond of him and showered him with lavish gifts, from satin shirts to well-honed blades and fiery steeds. Inside the palace, all was luxury and ease. Food and ale were plentiful, for there were cauldrons in the palace which never became empty, and musicians serenaded the couple wherever they went. At other times, Oisin went out hunting in the fields and forests, testing his skills against many a boar or deer. And, throughout

all this time, he felt neither pain nor sickness. Indeed, he was not a day older than that moment when he first set foot in Niamh's native land.

Oisin spent three happy years in this fashion in Tir na nÓg. Then, at last, he felt a great urge to see Finn and his old companions once more. So he went to Niamh and told her of his desire to pay them a visit. She looked sad, when he gave her this news. 'You must go if you wish, my husband, though it grieves me to say it. For the journey is long, and I feel in my heart that I will never see you again.'

But Oisin would not be dissuaded. 'Surely, if you lend me your magic steed,' he said, 'I will cross the seas in no time at all.'

'Very well,' agreed Niamh, 'but you must promise me this. Be sure that you do not climb down from the horse's back. If your feet touch the soil of Ireland, you will never return to Tir na nÓg.'

Oisin consented to this and made ready to leave. Soon, the preparations were complete and he bade farewell to Niamh. Tears streamed down her face as she kissed him goodbye and, for a fleeting moment, he was tempted to stay. But then he remembered his happy childhood days at Almu, surrounded by Finn and the warriors of the Fianna, and he convinced himself that a short visit could do no harm and that he would not be parted for long from his beloved.

So, mounting up, he turned the horse towards the sea and galloped off into the misty air. The journey was just as wonderful as it had been before, with strange sights and spectacles that he could not explain. Then, before too long, he saw the grassy plains of Ireland appearing in the distance. Eagerly, Oisin rode ashore and headed for Almu. As he travelled, however, he began to feel uneasy, for it seemed to him that everything was strangely altered. He saw none of the imposing figures of the Fianna hunting on his father's land, as they had always done. Instead, the people that he passed looked small and sickly. Perhaps, he thought, the answer will become clear at Almu itself.

Speeding on his way, Oisin soon came to the hill where his former home had stood. There, a cruel sight awaited him. Almu was no more. Where once the towers of Finn's palace had loomed high and mighty, now there were only grassy mounds, covered with weeds and bracken. Mystified, Oisin called out his father's name; then he called out for Conan Mail, for Ficna and for Mac Luga of the Red Hand; he even shouted for Finn's hounds, Bran and Sceolan. Nothing. The only sounds that could be heard were the murmuring of the breeze and the cawing of the rooks.

So Oisin turned his horse around and headed east, towards Glenasmole. There, he came upon a group of peasants, who were struggling to move a boulder. These people seemed as puny as the others that Oisin had seen. They, for their part, were amazed to see a man so huge and powerful. With a common voice they called out to him and asked for his assistance, thinking that it would be no great task for a man of his stature to shift the obstacle.

Obligingly, Oisin trotted over to them and stooped down from his horse, to put his weight behind the stone. He moved it with ease, but the manoeuvre was an awkward one and he felt himself losing his balance. With a desperate lunge, he tried to grab the horse's neck, but it was too late. Seconds later, he had tumbled down and was lying on the ground. Immediately, the horse reared up and shook its mane. Then, wheeling round, it galloped away at full speed and no one could stop it.

Oisin did not have time to run after it, for a terrible transformation was beginning to afflict him. The strength ebbed away from his limbs, his eyes grew dim and his voice became feeble. In a matter of moments, he turned into a weak and decrepit man. The people of Glenasmole stared open-mouthed at this spectacle, not knowing what to make of it. Then one of them noticed that Oisin was trying to speak.

'Take me to Finn,' he implored in a frail voice. 'He will understand this enchantment and know how to cure it.'

But, to Oisin's horror, his words were only received with mirth. 'Did you say Finn, old man? Why, your wits must be addled. For Finn has been dead these three hundred years, and all the heroes of the Fianna with him.' Then Oisin began to understand the secret of Tir na nÓg, and it brought him to the edge of despair. Time had indeed stood still for him in the Land of Youth. For, though it seemed to him that he had been absent for just three years, the world of men had moved on by three centuries. And, in all this time, he himself had not aged by so much as a day. Only when his link with the magical land was broken did the years leave their mark upon him.

Seeing his distress, the people of Glenasmole brought Oisin before St Patrick, confident that he would know what should be done. The holy man treated Oisin kindly and hospitably, offering him food and shelter. Then he tried to explain how Ireland had changed during his absence; how Christianity had come to the land and the old gods had withered away. Oisin lamented loudly when he heard these things, remembering all the happy days that he had enjoyed with the Fianna. Patrick listened with interest to these tales and instructed his scribes to copy them down, so that Ireland should know of its ancient heroes.

Oisin remained with Patrick and his priests, for he had nowhere else to go. They looked after him, tending to his aching limbs and trying to console him with the teachings of the Gospel. Oisin listened indulgently, but his mind was elsewhere. Until the end of his days, he never ceased to yearn for the feasts at Almu and the rousing hunts in the wild forests; for the friendship of Finn and the lost companions of his youth; and, most of all, for the love of his gentle Niamh of the Golden Hair, whom he would never see again.

123

Glossary and Pronunciation Guide

The following glossary contains a pronunciation guide, indicated in brackets. This is a general guide only and will provide an accessible interpretation of the main characters and place-names used in this book.

Aife (ee-fe) – Sister of Scáthach and lover of Cú Chulainn

Ailill (ai-lil) – (i) Medb's consort, the King of Connacht (*The Cattle Raid of Cooley*); (ii) Father of Etain and King of Ulster (*The Wooing of Etain*)

Ailill Anglonnach (ai-lil anghlo-nack) – Brother of Eochaid Airem, in love with Etain (*The Wooing of Etain*)

Aillen (ahl-en) – Fire-breathing demon, defeated by Finn

Aobh (ay-ov) – Foster-daughter of Bodb and mother of the children of Lir

Aoife (ee-fa) – (i) The wicked step-mother of Lir's children (*The Fate of the Children of Lir*); (ii) The lover of Ilbrec; she is transformed into a crane (*The Boyhood of Finn*)

Boann (boh-ann) – A water goddess and mother of Oenghus; the River Boyne is named after her

Bodb (bove) – Son of the Dagda and his successor as leader of the Tuatha Dé Danaan

Brí Leith (bree leyth) – Home of Midir the Proud

Brug na Bóinne (broo neh boyne) – Prehistoric tomb complex at Newgrange; also one of the Sidhe

Caer (kay-r) – Lover of Oenghus

Conchobar (kon-cho-var) – King of Ulster during the cattle raid of Cooley

Conn (kon) – (i) One of the children of Lir (*The Fate of the Children of Lir*); (ii) Conn of the Hundred Battles, a high king of Ireland (*The Boyhood of Finn*)

Connacht (kon-act) – The old name for the county of Connaught; its people, the Connachta, were thought to be descendants of Conn of the Hundred Battles

Connla (kon-la) – Son of Cú Chulainn and Aife

Cú Chulainn (ku hull-in or ku cull-in) – The supreme warrior in the Ulster army, the Hound of Ulster

Cumhal (coom-hal) – Finn's father

Dagda (thag-fa) – The father of the gods

Deirdre (der-dra) – Also known as Deirdre of the Sorrows; she elopes with Naoise

Eochaid Airem (yochi ahrem) – High king; husband of Etain

Emain Macha (evin maka) – Ulster's chief stronghold in ancient times

Emer (ay-ver) – Cú Chulainn's wife

Etain (ay-tin) – Daughter of Ailill; loved by Midir the Proud and Eochaid Airem

Fand (fandh) – Wife of Manannán Mac Lir and lover of Cú Chulainn

Ferdia (fir-dia) – Friend of Cú Chulainn, now enlisted in the Connacht army

Fergus Mac Roth (fergus mok roth) – Exiled Ulsterman, fighting in Medb's army

Fianna (fee-ana) – Elite band of warriors, led by Finn

Finn Mac Cumhal (fin mok coom-hal) – Leader of the Fianna and hero of the Fionn cycle

Firbolg (fur-bolg) – Race of invaders

Fomorians (fo-moor-ians) – Vicious race of sea pirates

Ilbrec (ill-brek) – Ruler of the Sidh of Assaroe; a contender for the Dagda's crown

Lia Fáil (lea fayl) – Coronation stone of the high kings at Tara

Laeg (loygh) – Cú Chulainn's charioteer

Lir (leer) – Sea god, father of the children of Lir and of the sea god Manannán Mac Lir

Lochlann (lock-lan) – Distant northern land, usually identified with Norway

Lugh (loo) – Sun god and father of Cú Chulainn

Lughnasadh (loo-nes-ah) – Celtic summer festival held on August 1, named after Lugh

Macha (maka) – War goddess, lays a curse on the Ulstermen

Mac Roth (mok roth) – Medb's herald

Manannán Mac Lir (manan-awn mok leer) – Powerful sea god, traditionally cited as the first king of the Isle of Man

Medb (mayv) – Queen of Connacht, who wages war against Ulster

Midac (my-thack) – Survivor of a defeated army, fostered by Finn

Midir (midge-her) – Midir the Proud, foster-father of Oenghus and suitor of Etain

Muirne (mew-ern) – Finn's mother

Muirthemne, Plain of (mew-them-nyeh) – Cú Chulainn's homeland, now associated with the area around Dundalk

Naoise (nee-sha) – The son of Usnach, who elopes with Deirdre

Niamh (neev) – Oisin's lover, a princess of Tir na nÓg

Oenghus (engus) – Son of the Dagda; the god of love

Oisin (usheen) – Son of Finn and leading warrior of the Fianna

Sadb (sighve) – Finn's wife, the mother of Oisin

Samhain (saavin) – Celtic festival, held on 1 November

Scáthach (skaw-thach) – Supernatural female warrior; Cú Chulainn's military trainer

Síd Finnachaid (shee finna-kad) – Home of Lir

Sidhe (shee) – The fairy mounds, invisible to men, where the gods have their homes

Tuatha Dé Danaan (tua day dhanna) – The ancient gods of Ireland

Tuiren (tir-en) – Finn's half-sister

Uchtdealb (uck-they-alv) – Uchtdealb of the Fair Breast, a fairy woman who turns Tuiren into a hound

Uí Néill (y nail) – Powerful Ulster tribe, said to be descended from an ancient king, Niall of the Nine Hostages

Ullan Eachtach (oolan y-atack) – A member of the Fianna, husband of Tuiren

Usnach (oosnack) – Son-in-law of Cathbad the Druid; his sons are tragically led astray by Deirdre

Bibliography

Berresford Ellis, P,
Dictionary of Celtic Mythology, Constable, 1992

Chadwick, Nora,
The Celts, Pelican, 1970

Cross T P & Slover C,
Ancient Irish Tales, George G Harrap, 1936

Dillon, Myles,
Early Irish Literature, Cambridge University Press, 1948

Faraday, Winifred,
The Cattle Raid of Cualnge, David Nutt, 1904

Gantz, Jeffrey,
Early Irish Myths and Sagas (trans.), Penguin, 1981

Green, Miranda,
Dictionary of Celtic Myth and Legend,
Thames & Hudson, 1992

Gregory, Lady Augusta,
Cuchullin of Muirthemne, John Murray, 1902

Gregory, Lady Augusta,
Gods and Fighting Men, John Murray, 1904

Harbison, Peter,
Pre-Christian Ireland, Thames & Hudson, 1988

Hull, Eleanor,
A Text Book of Irish Literature, David Nutt, 1906

Jackson, Kenneth,
A Celtic Miscellany (trans.), Penguin, 1971

Joyce, P W,
Old Celtic Romances, David Nutt, 1894

Kinsella, Thomas,
The Táin (trans.), Oxford University Press, 1969

Knott, Eleanor & Murphy, Gerard,
Early Irish Literature, Routledge & Kegan, 1966

Leahy, A L,
Heroic Romances of Ireland, David Nutt, 1905

Rolleston, T W,
Celtic Myths and Legends, Senate, 1994 (reprint)

Sharkey, John,
Celtic Mysteries, Thames & Hudson, 1975

Yeats, W B,
Writings on Irish Folklore, Legend and Myth, Penguin, 1993

Picture Credits

Wherever possible, the Publishers have attempted to contact the copyright holders of the images reproduced in this book.

Front cover: Lower Lough Erne, County Fermanagh, Northern Ireland (© David Lyons); inset: Gold boat from the Broighter hoard (© National Museum of Ireland, Dublin) Spine: Iron Age spear (The British Museum, London/Werner Forman Archive).

Page 1, Bronze vessel (© National Museum of Ireland, Dublin); page 2, Carved stone head on Boa Island, Lower Lough Erne, County Fermanagh, Northern Ireland (© David Lyons); page 5, Bronze figurines of boars (The British Museum, London/Werner Forman Archive); page 6, The Broighter Torc (© National Museum of Ireland, Dublin); page 7, Bronze openwork chariot-mount (Rheinisches Landesmuseum, Bonn); page 8, Bronze scabbard (© Trustees of the National Museums of Scotland); page 9, Hill of Ushnagh, Westmeath, Ireland (© David Lyons); page 10, Three-faced stone head of a Celtic deity, Corleck, County Cavan, Ireland (© National Museum of Ireland, Dublin); page 11, Initial letter from the Book of Kells; page 13, Carpet page of St John's Gospel, Lindisfarne Gospels, Cott Nero D IV fol. 211 (British Library, London/The Bridgeman Art Library, London); pages 14–15, View across Long Range, between Muckross Lake and Upper Lake, Killarney, County Kerry, Ireland (© David Lyons); page 16, Bronze harness mount, South Shields Roman fort (Museum of Antiquities of the University and Society of Antiquaries of Newcastle upon Tyne); page 17, Figure of Venus (© Museum of London); page 18, The Snettisham Torc (The British Museum, London/Ancient Art and Architecture Collection); page 19, above: Bronze disc, Monasterevin, County Kildare, Ireland (© National Museum of Ireland, Dublin), below: Bronze disc, Lambay Island, County Dublin, Ireland (© National Museum of Ireland, Dublin); page 20, Detail of Evangelist symbols, fol. 129 v., Book of Kells; page 22, The Mound of the Hostages, Tara, County Meath, Ireland (© David Lyons); page 23, Entrance stone, Newgrange, Ireland (C M Dixon);

page 25, Bronze figure of a female (Musée Historique d'Orléanais, Orléans); page 27, Detail of a fragment from a bell shrine (National Museum of Ireland, Dublin/© R Sheridan, Ancient Art and Architecture Collection); page 28, The Battersea Shield (© The British Museum, London); page 29, The Lewis Chessmen (© The British Museum, London); page 30, Figure of a horse (Rheinisches Landesmuseum, Trier); page 31, Bronze flagon (Rheinisches Landesmuseum, Bonn); page 32, Iron fire-dog in the shape of a horned bull (The British Museum, London/Werner Forman Archive); page 33, Pictish symbol stone, Scotland (C M Dixon); page 34, Bronze sword (Musée des Antiquités Nationales, St Germain-en-Laye/Lauros-Giraudon); page 35, Bronze pig (Commissioners of Public Works, Dublin); page 37, Gold boat from the Broighter hoard (© National Museum of Ireland, Dublin); page 39, Iron Age spear with bronze decoration (The British Museum, London/Werner Forman Archive); page 40, Gold weight (© R Sheridan, Ancient Art and Architecture Collection); page 42, Stone font, Clonfert Cathedral, County Galway, Ireland (© David Lyons); page 43, Miniature of St Brendan and a siren, St Brendan Codex (Heidelberg University Library, Germany/The Bridgeman Art Library, London); page 44, Venus and Nymphs, High Rochester (Museum of Antiquities of the University and Society of Antiquaries of Newcastle upon Tyne); page 45, Clay figure of a Romano-Celtic fertility goddess (© The British Museum, London); page 47, Detail of a bronze flesh-hook, County Antrim, Ireland (C M Dixon); page 48, Slieve League, County Donegal, Ireland (© David Lyons); page 50, Engraved bronze terminal in the shape of a swan's head (© Trustees of the National Museums of Scotland); page 52, Detail from the Gundestrup Cauldron (Danish National Museum/E T Archive); page 53, Bronze figure of an animal-god (© R Sheridan, Ancient Art and Architecture Collection); page 55, Crucifixion, Southampton Psalter (Geoffrey Goode/Book Creation Services); pages 56–57, Caherdorgan North Stone Fort, Dingle Peninsula, County Kerry, Ireland (© David Lyons); page 58, Bronze brooch in the form of a collared bird (Keltenmuseum, Hallein/AKG London/Erich

Acknowledgements

I am very grateful for all the support and advice which I have received from friends and colleagues. In particular, I would like to express my thanks to Valmai Adams, Peter Berry, Ian Chilvers, Diane Dewar, Peter Herzog, Caroline Juler, Daphne Miller, Elizabeth Peart, Michael Sherborne, Sue Talbot, Hat Visick and Yayoi Yamaguchi.

The publishers would like to thank Mandy Greenfield and Kate Yeates for their invaluable help.